THIS BOOK

BELONGS TO:

_____

_____

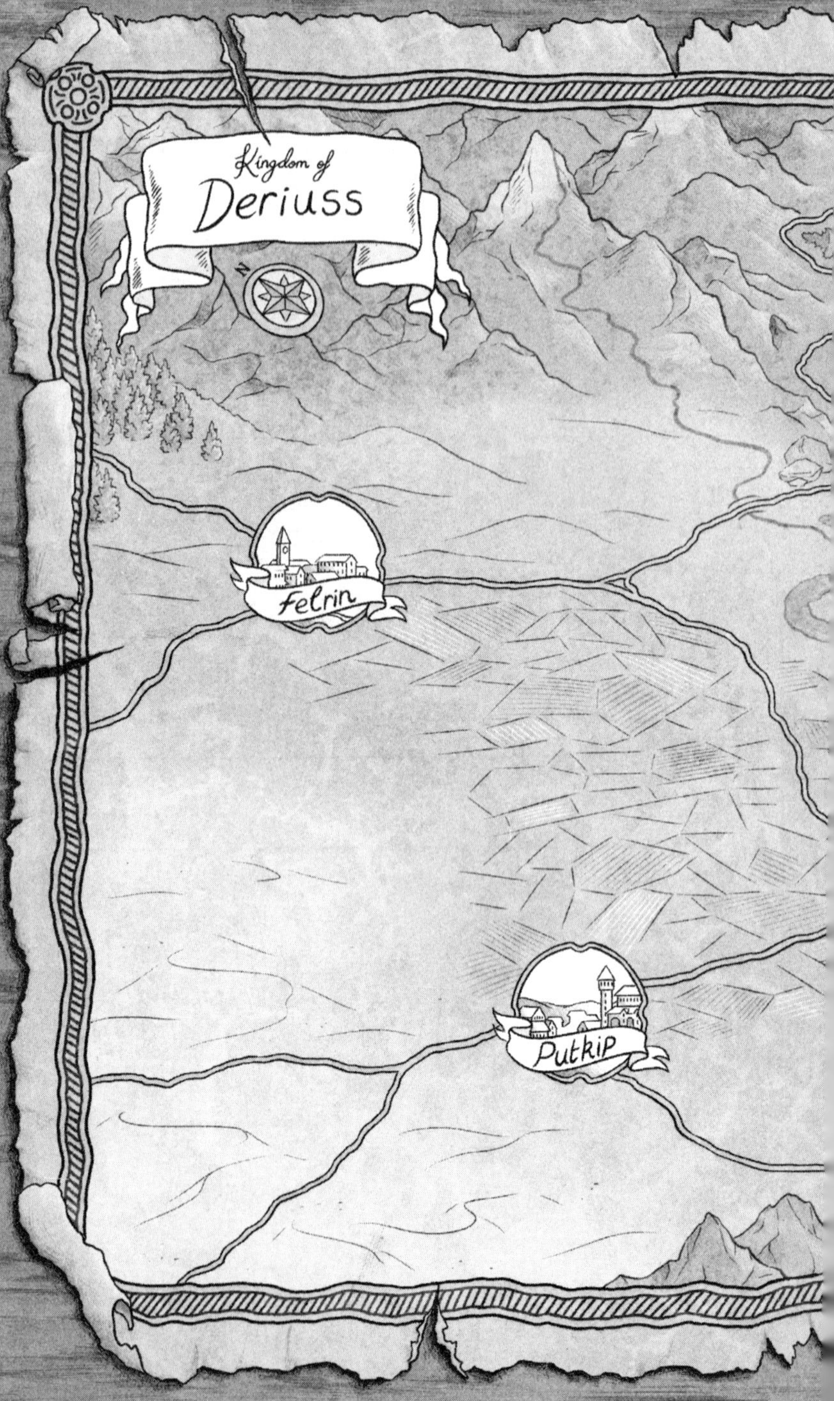
Kingdom of
Deriuss
Felrin
Putkip

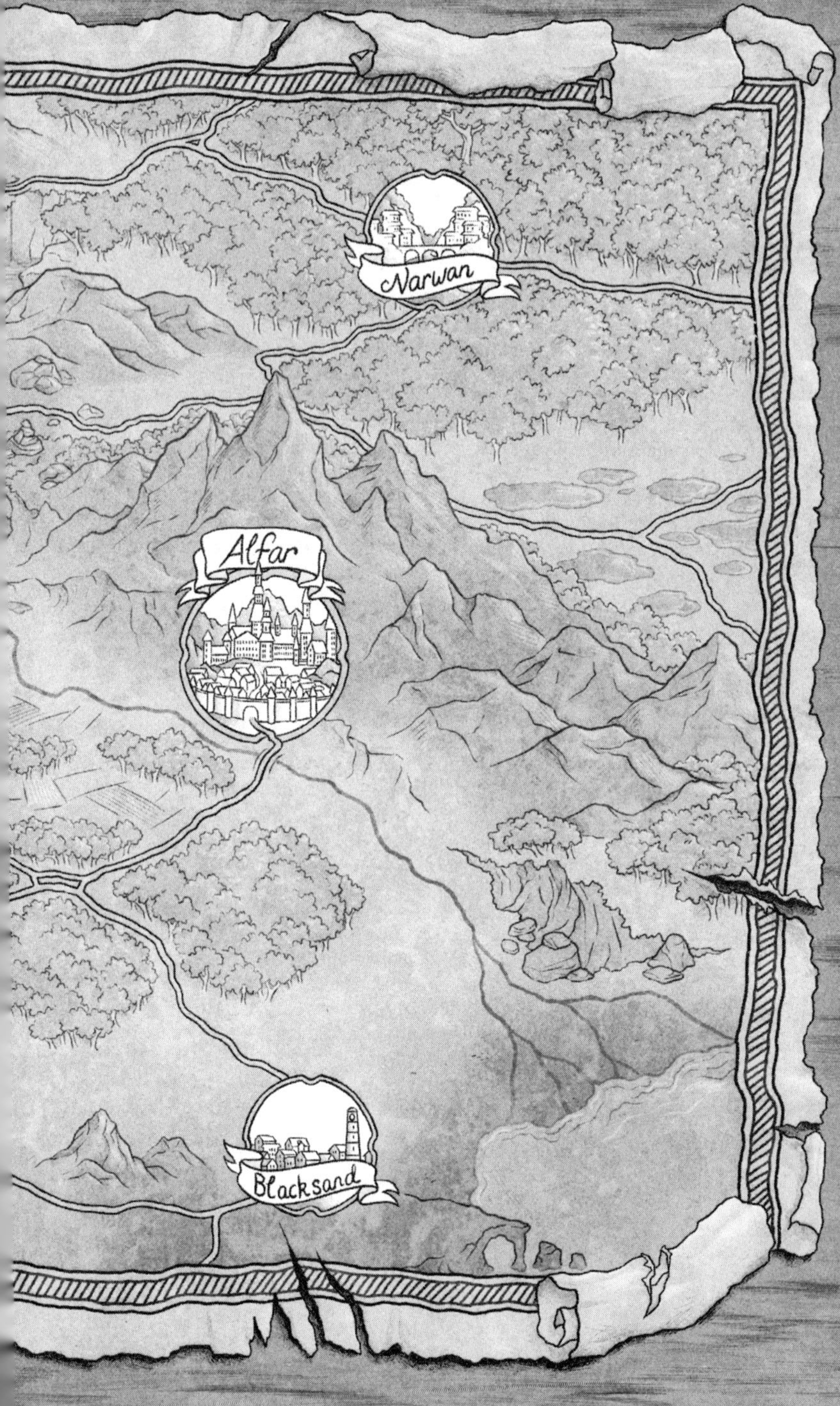
Narwan
Alfar
Blacksand

First published 2020 © Twinkl Ltd of Wards Exchange,
197 Ecclesall Road, Sheffield S11 8HW

ISBN: 978-1-8381906-1-3

Printed in the United Kingdom.

10 9 8 7 6 5 4 3 2 1

A catalogue record for this book is available from the British Library.

A TWINKL ORIGINAL

COLE'S KINGDOM

Twinkl Educational Publishing

CONTENTS

CHAPTER ONE
GRANDMA'S ATTIC

The final, twisted road to Grandma Jenny's house was the most exciting and the most terrifying part of the journey. The rough track snaked up the steep hillside as trees loomed heavily, their leafy fingers scraping against the windows of the car. Tyres crunched loose gravel and brittle twigs while the engine groaned. Pressed into the middle seat, Cole bounced up and down, squashed between his big brother and little sister.

"It's a bit like a journey to another world, isn't it?" said Cole, craning over his sister, Mara, to catch a glimpse of Grandma Jenny's house through the trees. "It's like a window through time…"

"I'm trying to sleep," said Liam, as Dad swung the car

round a tight bend, causing the wheels to skid.

Cole ignored his brother. "I mean, Grandma Jenny's house must be a hundred years old at least. It's so crumbly."

"Nearly three hundred," Mum corrected.

"She doesn't have a proper TV, either – just that boxy thing, and her phone is stuck to the wall. I mean, it has buttons! It's like she lives in a museum."

"Well, don't tell Grandma that, for goodness' sake," said Mum. "You'll hurt her feelings."

"They didn't even have TVs three hundred years ago," Mara scoffed without looking up from her book. "Even I know that, and I'm not even in high school yet." Cole had only been three years old when he had been adopted into the family but, for as long as he could remember, Mara had always been too clever for her own good. Now that she was nine and he was eleven, she never missed a chance to make him look foolish.

"Yeah, *thanks*, Mara," said Cole.

"You're welcome, Cole." She smiled in the least friendly way possible.

Cole was about to respond with something that he knew would get him into trouble when, out of the corner of his eye, he spotted the house on the hill. "Look! There it is."

"Hey! Get off," said Liam, as Cole threw himself sideways to peer out of the window. Through the trees, Cole could see the dark stone and pointed gables of Grandma Jenny's house. She'd lived there ever since she was a little girl but soon, she would be leaving forever.

Grandma Jenny was nearly eighty. Her hands trembled and her knees quaked. These days, when she made a cup of tea, she only filled it halfway so as not to spill it and, when she tackled the stairs, more often than not, the stairs won. That was why she was moving out of her narrow, wonky old house and coming to live with Cole and his family.

After another bumpy minute, the car pulled to a stop outside the imposing front door. There was no one there to welcome them; the house looked as though it were asleep, the curtains drawn against the sunlight. Until recently, Grandma Jenny would greet the family from the front step the moment they arrived. She would fling out her arms so that her three grandchildren could run for a lavender-scented cuddle and a scratchy kiss.

"I want you all on your best behaviour, all right?" said Mum as they climbed from the car. "Your grandma doesn't need you running or shouting or moaning. This is a sad day for her, packing up her belongings to leave the house that she's lived in for so long. So *be nice.*"

"But why have we got to help?" Liam complained as they unloaded empty cardboard boxes from the boot. "I've got to practise, you know." Not content with having recently won the county swimming championship, Liam had also just earned his Grade 5 saxophone and was now learning to play the guitar. Mum had once asked Cole if he would like to learn to play an instrument, but he knew that this particular achievement, like many others, was already taken.

"Please don't tell me that I have to listen to any more of your 'music'," Mara moaned. "There's only so much clanging and clattering and squealing I can take."

"You can work with me if you like," Cole offered. "We'll go to the spare room – you remember, the one with the spider webs big enough to catch whole birds? There'll be goblins under the bed and ghosts in the sheets –"

"No, thank you," said Mara. "You're always telling tales."

"How about we pack up the study?" said Mum. "We can decide which books to keep."

"That's more like it!" Mara grabbed her bag and sprang up the steps to the front door. Cole suspected that Mara would spend all day reading rather than helping. For someone who loved books, she couldn't stand it when Cole came up with his own unique brand of story.

Inside the house, Grandma Jenny was sitting in her usual green armchair, a cold cup of tea on the table beside her. She looked smaller and paler than the last time the family had visited, almost swamped by the intricately patterned blanket drawn over her knees. It bore tiny images of outdoor scenes, all woven together like a collage. She wrapped herself in it even on the hottest of summer days and, even though it looked old and weathered, it was still soft to the touch. It was her armour. She dozed, so Cole woke her up by resting his warm hand on her wrinkled one.

"Hiya, Grandma."

"Cole? Is that you?" said Grandma Jenny, waking slowly and blinking to bring the world into focus. Her grey eyes were still bright. "Give us a kiss and a cup of tea. I don't mind which comes first." Cole stooped to plant a kiss on Grandma's cheek, and she grinned. "Kiss it is! Now, tell me everything that you've been up to since I last saw you."

Once the rest of the family had greeted Grandma and begun to traipse through the house with empty bags, boxes and suitcases to fill, Cole told Grandma Jenny about his friend, Leo, and his birthday party at the trampoline centre that had ended with a trip to A&E and Leo's arm in plaster. He told her about his new English teacher who started every class by reciting a sonnet. He told her about how their cat had got herself stuck in the next-door neighbour's tree and how he had climbed the tree to fetch her down.

Grandma smiled and nodded and asked questions in all the right places. She was the only person who never got bored when Cole told his stories. He knew that he wasn't accomplished like Liam or brainy like Mara, but he was what his headmistress would call 'a chatterbox'.

"...and she was yowling the whole time I was carrying her down. It was like this." Cole yowled long and loud. "She scratched my shoulder a lot, but I didn't mind. I just wanted her to be safe."

"Cole," said Mum, "we're dying of thirst out here." She brought in another armload of empty boxes from the car, her face beaded with sweat. "Stop talking Grandma's ear off. Could you get us something to drink, please?"

"Oops. Sorry, Grandma," said Cole, scrambling from his perch on the arm of Grandma's chair.

"No need to apologise," said Grandma as Cole hurried to the kitchen and hastily poured five cups of tea and an orange squash for Mara.

Armed with refreshments, the family split up to pack different parts of the house. Mum and Mara took the study, Liam was sent to pack instruments in the music room and Dad would start with the shed – the dirtiest job of all.

"...and Cole." Grandma turned to him, her eyes sparkling. "How do you fancy going into the attic? It's full of all manner of treasures, you know."

"Is it?" Cole asked, breathless. "I've never been in the attic before. Are there spiders? I've read a book about spiders and they're really interesting creatures. Did you know that there's a spider who lives in my wardrobe?" Cole cradled his tea and rocked a little on the balls of his feet. "Are you sure that's where you want me to go? I won't know what to do with the treasures, Grandma. I'll probably just break them or throw out the wrong thing."

"Don't worry, my dear. You are the right person for the job."

"What if there are ghosts or wolves or tiny trolls in the dust?" asked Cole. "I don't mind ghosts, as long as they're friendly, but I want to be prepared."

Grandma chuckled. "You'll be fine. If you find anything valuable, I'll know that it's in safe hands."

Cole had never thought about his hands being safe. They certainly weren't that safe when he played rugby at school – at least, that's what his teacher, Mr Evans, had said.

"Mind you don't trip over the beams," Grandma was saying. Then, from under her blanket, she pulled a small, silver keyring. "You'll be needing these."

Cole gripped the keys tightly in one hand and tucked an empty cardboard box under his other arm. As he climbed the stairs towards the attic, the voices of his family drifted through the house. Mara was deep into a book and Mum was telling her off.

"But how will I know if it's worth keeping it if I don't read it to check?"

Dad was clattering around in the kitchen, cursing, having apparently stubbed his toe on something in the shed. Somewhere on the top floor, Liam was twanging an out-of-tune guitar and singing along to his own made-up song.

"*Now, I'm stuck in this dusty old house, pretty sure I just saw a mouse...*"

At the end of the second-floor landing was a narrow staircase that led to the attic room. The stairs were uncarpeted and the floral wallpaper was yellowed and falling away from the wall in strips. Cole clutched the keys tightly as he climbed the creaking steps.

He had never been in Grandma Jenny's attic. When they were younger, he, Mara and Liam had often begged to be allowed up there to explore or play games, but Grandma had always said that it wasn't 'tidy enough'. Now, she had trusted Cole to finish tidying for her and he was going to do his absolute best – dust trolls or no dust trolls.

The door at the top of the stairs was smaller and narrower than a normal door and the keyhole looked ancient. Cole stared at the two keys in his hand and chose the oldest-looking one but, when he jammed it into the rusty keyhole, nothing happened. Selecting the second of the two, he renewed his efforts. It took a little wiggling and jiggling to get the key to turn but, when Cole put his shoulder to the door, it swung open with a heavy *clunk*, shredding stubborn cobwebs as it went.

The attic was long and gloomy and filled with mixed-up shapes and threatening angles. Light seeped in from three grimy skylights and the air swam with dust. Fresh rain tapped its fingertips on the roof and wind whipped through the trees outside. Cole felt very far away from everyone, as if the world and everything in it were trapped within the attic itself. He stuffed Grandma Jenny's keys into his pocket and fumbled around the doorway until he found an old-fashioned light switch on a chain. When he pulled, a smattering of ancient bulbs in ornate light fittings blinked on.

"Woah," Cole breathed.

He had expected mouldy boxes and bags full of old clothes and toys, like his family's attic at home, but, as he stepped closer, he saw that Grandma's could not have been more different.

Cole was standing on the edge of what looked like a model town made up of the strangest collection of objects he had ever seen, piled up in towers and heaps with narrow avenues of floorboard between them. There were cupboards and dressers made of dark wood with leaves and flowers carved into their grain. When Cole opened their drawers, he found them stuffed full: silver tankards and brass candlesticks and ancient, hard-backed books with golden, stamped titles. Cole opened a large chest filled with clothes that looked like they came from Victorian times. Then, he opened a small chest and found row upon row of large, dangling earrings arranged on a cushioned tray. He was going to need a bigger box.

He brushed by an old rocking horse and set it swinging back and forth, its white mane swishing. "There, boy. Shh, now." He stroked the horse's ears until it became still, as though it were real. He knew that it was silly, but he felt like he was trespassing in a sleeping world. He was nervous in case he woke anything that shouldn't be disturbed.

As he picked his way around the attic, his eyes slid over oil paintings, porcelain dolls, ornate vases, a rusty bicycle and a leather saddle. Stepping closer to inspect a carved, wooden mirror with a gilded handle, Cole almost tripped over something soft on the ground.

He crouched to look. A tangle of faded fabric was sitting on the dusty floorboards and, even among this strange array of objects, it looked out of place. As Cole mused, a sparkle of light called out to him from the centre of the fabric nest. He pulled at it cautiously, revealing what looked like a piece of fine jewellery snuggled tightly inside.

The strange object was a metal disc a little bigger than Cole's palm. It was made of gleaming gold, shaped into an intricate pattern and encrusted with dazzling jewels. When he stared into the precious stones, Cole could swear that they twirled and danced inside themselves. There were four in total, each a different colour: green, yellow, orange and blue. Fascinated, Cole set about running his thumb over each jewel to remove the fine layer of dust coating them.

The effect upon Cole's senses when his skin touched the blue stone was immediate, and it knocked him backwards in surprise. He felt cold and tremendously hungry; his shoulders gave a violent shiver and he whipped his hand away. Breathing hard, he placed a finger over the green stone, and was immediately warmed by an inexplicable surge of hopefulness and a breeze which ruffled his hair. The brooch-like ornament was both heavy and weightless and he knew that, above all the other things he had seen in the attic, this was the most precious of all Grandma's possessions.

"What *is* this?"

Lost in the wondrous artefact, Cole did not hear the sound of scurrying claws on the floorboards until it was too late. Before he knew what was happening, tiny teeth had sunk into his finger and thieving furry fingers had grabbed the brooch from his hands.

"Ouch! What – *what?*"

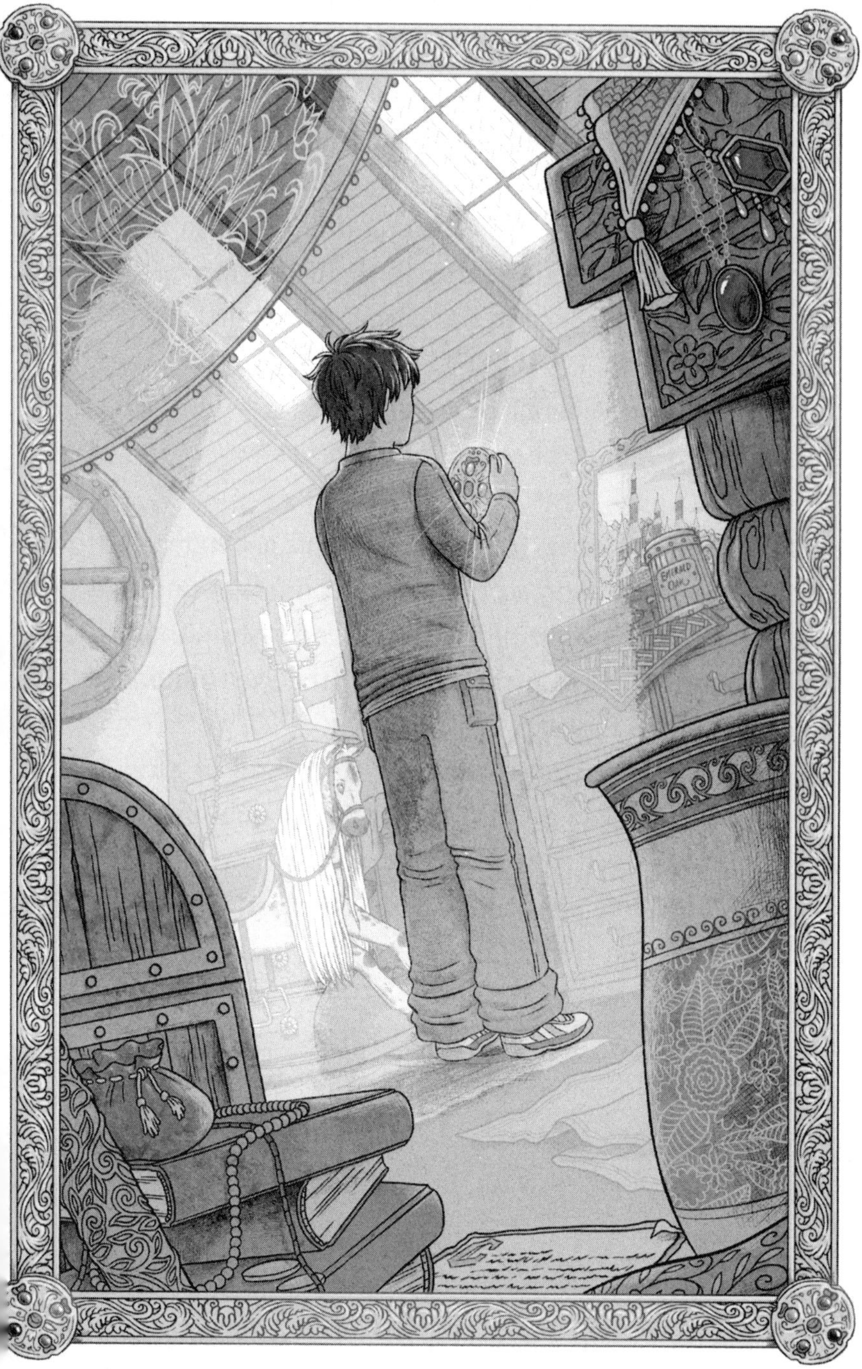

Cole wasn't quite sure what he was seeing. It had the rounded, white ears and thin, pointed tail of a mouse, but was tall enough that its feet made an audible patter on the floorboards as it ran. The creature clung to the golden brooch and tore a path through the collection of treasures towards a dank space in the corner of the attic.

"Hey! Come back here." Cole blinked hard – was it his eyes, or had that mouse been wearing *clothes*?

Cole dashed after it. He skidded round a bend, leapt over an expensive-looking statue of a sleeping lion and was just in time to catch sight of the mouse, now standing tall and triumphant, next to a small hole in the skirting board.

It turned to Cole and squeaked, "On behalf of King Enk of Alfar, ruler of the land of Deriuss, I give you our thanks."

Then, it blew a particularly high-pitched raspberry and scuttled off into the hole.

CHAPTER TWO
THE SEAL OF FELRIN

Cole crouched next to the skirting board and peered through the hole. A dry heat blew from the darkness, making his eyes water. He had expected to see nothing but wooden beams and crumbling plaster, or else get splashed by the rain coming down hard from outside. However, as his vision cleared, he spied a long tunnel ending in a pale, white light and the mouse bounding into the distance. Was there another room there?

Without stopping to wonder how, Cole plunged first a finger, then a hand, then his whole body into the strange space that seemed to grow around him. The tunnel was cramped and smelled of damp earth, and Cole crawled like a caterpillar until he felt sunlight hitting his face. Determined to escape the narrow tunnel into whatever room lay behind the attic wall, he scrambled up the last few feet and pushed himself off the ground. Breathing heavily, he looked around him, and what he saw made his jaw drop.

"Wh-what?"

He was standing in a brittle, blackened forest. The ground was hard and cracked, and the trees were tall and bare. A scorching, white sun blazed down over everything, baking rocks and plants alike, and Cole could see no buildings or people at all.

Shock and panic flooded through him. Staring in every direction, he forced himself to blink but, after reopening his eyes for the third time and seeing no change in the scenery, he was forced to accept that he really was standing outdoors, in what seemed to be a very hot country – and Grandma Jenny's house was nowhere to be seen.

The heat burned Cole's skin through his thin jumper and he started to sweat. Breathing hard, he whirled round to peer back through the tunnel, but saw that the hole from which he had emerged was now nothing more than a shadowy gap between the dry tree roots. Where *was* he? Where was Grandma Jenny's attic and, more importantly, how would he get back?

Just as Cole began to feel a ball of fear welling up in his throat, a sudden eruption of dust disturbed the still air. Cole spun on the spot. "Hey!"

The mouse, which was easily the size of a large cat, was shaking the dust and dirt out of its tunic behind a nearby tree. At Cole's words, it jumped and bounded off through the trees, kicking up miniature whirlwinds with each hop. Cole followed in its wake but his trainers slipped on the dusty ground.

"Wait!" he yelled desperately, sprinting uphill as fast as he could. "Come back!"

The mouse didn't slow.

"Please!" Cole was panting already. The slope was steep but the mouse bounded tirelessly upwards, clutching the strange, golden disc with its tail.

Cole felt powerless. Liam would have caught up with the mouse in the blink of an eye and Mara would have outsmarted the creature with a trap or a trick of her own. It was all that Cole could do to keep running and pleading. "Please, I need you to tell me what's going on!"

The mouse glanced backwards. "Leave this place, elseworlder! This seal doesn't belong to you!"

"Seal?" Cole puffed, picturing an animal with long whiskers

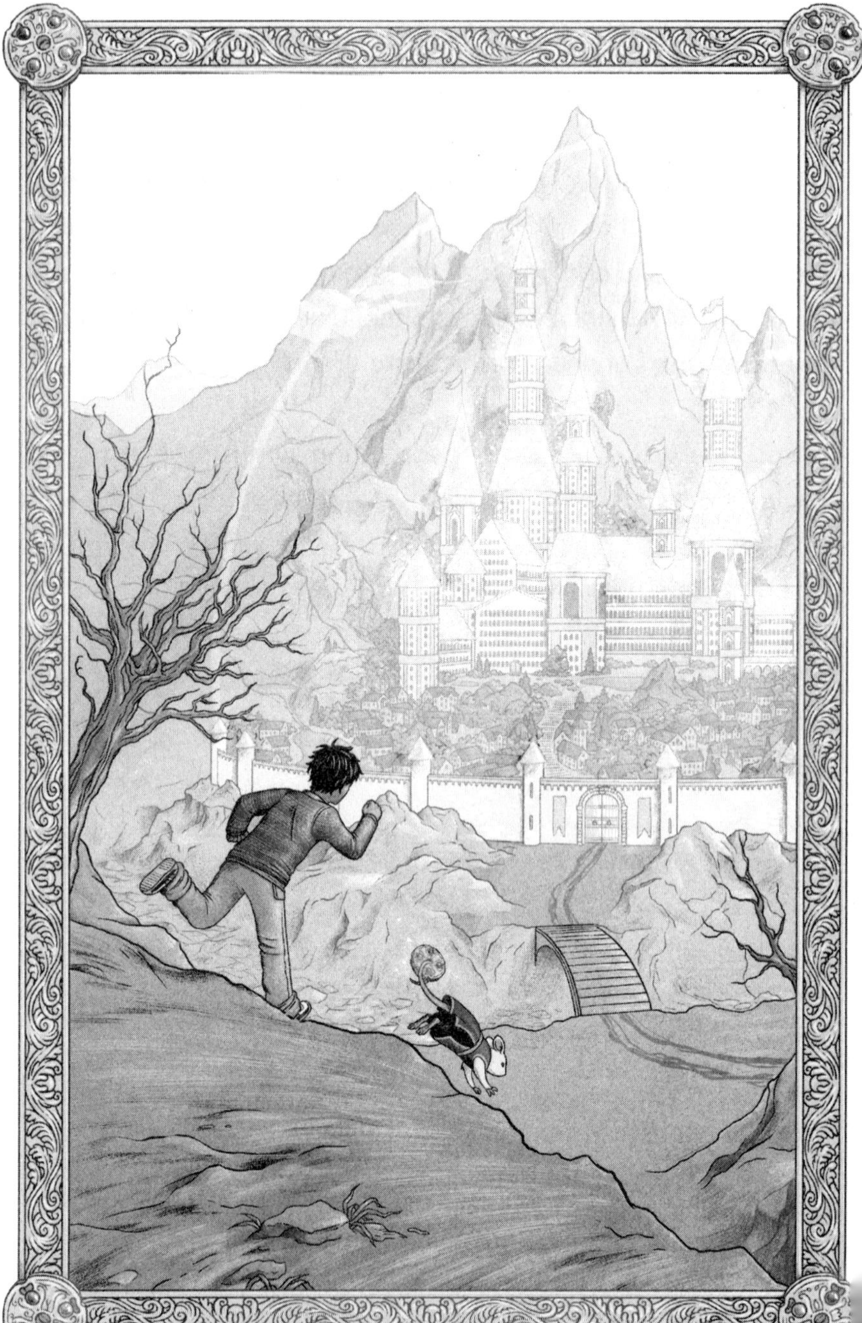

and a sopping wet nose.

"It belongs to the king." The mouse wasn't even out of breath. "His palace lies ahead. Take this as my one and only warning."

The heat dragged him down but Cole wasn't going to give up that easily. His heart thumped and his breath came in sharp gasps, but he pumped his arms and legs. Grandma Jenny had trusted him to keep safe anything that he thought was special, and her brooch was special, all right.

Up ahead, the trees thinned and the pair burst into a clearing dazzled by sunlight. On one side, the hillside fell away to reveal a vast valley with a sprawl of cottages and huts nestled at the bottom. On Cole's other side was a great white wall and a pair of enormous, ornately carved gates. The wall was twice as tall as Cole's school building and stretched around the face of the mountain so far that Cole thought that it must house an entire town at least. Above his head, beyond the wall, the towers of a palace made of pale marble reached into the sky, jutting from the mountain ridge like a snaggle-tooth. Pointy windows dotted the walls and the glass roofs swirled with dancing purple and green light. There were more turrets than Cole could count.

The sound of clanging bells cut through the air as the mouse ran the final paces to the gate. It stopped in the shadow of the towering structure and appeared to be waving its tiny paws. On the walkway above, a shadowy figure gestured back and then, with a slow groan, the gates were heaved open, revealing a dazzling aura of vibrant green and blue. Light spilled out onto the dry ground and the mouse stood defiant in its glow. Then, a tall figure the size of a man appeared, silhouetted between the gates, and advanced towards the mouse.

Gaining on the thief, Cole crossed the clearing as fast as his legs could carry him. His forehead was soaked with sweat and his muscles burned, but there was no way that he was going to let this mouse steal one of Grandma Jenny's belongings without so much as an explanation. As he closed in, the sound of the bells rang through his head louder and louder.

He was inches from the mouse when it bent into a deep bow and shouted, "A special delivery for the king: the seal of Felrin!"

"Give me that!" Cole spluttered, snatching up the shining object. Startled, the mouse gave a small squeak and turned to glare at him, but a sudden silence stopped them both in their tracks.

The bells had stopped ringing, and the shadow of the approaching figure fell over Cole. Looking up, he had to stifle a gasp.

An enormous white wolf was walking stiffly towards them on its hind legs. It was dressed in a breastplate and a red cape, which swished lazily around the creature's furred feet. Its eyes were a burning orange, and a glint around its mouth gave the merest suggestion of sharp fangs.

The wolf stopped directly in front of Cole and gazed down at him, amber eyes bulging. "Who is this?" she growled.

The mouse huffed. "Elseworlder." With a nervous glance at the newcomer, it scampered through the gates towards the palace, leaving them alone.

Cole held his breath as the wolf prowled around him in a circle, looking him up and down. She had long, grey streaks in the fur on her nose and, when her eyes fell on the object that the mouse had called 'the seal of Felrin', her gaze lingered and she smiled, revealing long, sharp teeth.

Cole clutched the circular ornament in both hands and it slipped and slid in his fingers, damp with sweat. The wolf was so close to his face that he could smell the hot stench of meaty breath.

"The king will be most pleased," she said. Her tone was soft but Cole could still hear a dangerous rumble hidden under the words. "Follow me."

Suddenly, she was marching off towards the castle gates and, to Cole's amazement, so was he. He didn't remember making the decision to follow his new and most unusual companion, but his feet seemed to have taken control of his actions. He pocketed the metal disc and exhaled slowly.

"It's OK," he muttered to himself. "It's all OK. It's a talking wolf. It's intelligent and won't eat you. It's probably just giving you a tour of the palace. It's fine."

As they passed under the arch of the gate, the most incredible phenomenon took place. The land through which he had sprinted minutes ago had been dry, cracked and dusty; there had been no signs of life and he had been sure that there could be no water for miles. No sooner had he passed under the great stone archway, however, than the ground beneath his feet turned luscious and green, and cool shade fell over his face.

"Oh, wow," Cole whispered.

The city inside the white walls burst with colour, light and sensations. Flowers of all kinds decorated the walls like a tapestry; marble pillars supported cool, shaded balconies and clear, crystalline pools filled stone basins. Mist from a nearby water feature speckled Cole's skin and he sighed as the thick layer of dust covering his body was swept away by a gentle breeze. Above everything towered the monumental palace with its marble turrets and, looking up, Cole saw soft, white clouds which seemed to vanish at the boundary wall as though trapped in this little oasis. It was, in every way, the complete opposite of the oppressive, stifling heat outside the palace walls.

"But..." he started, lost for words for the first time in his life. "I – but – *how*?"

Cole barely had time to register the well-dressed human inhabitants of the beautiful town before his host had led him up the central path through the town and onto a series of polished steps in the direction of the palace itself. He did a double take as two bowing badgers in blue tunics heaved the great doors open and, from there, it was a short walk down a gleaming hallway to a vast throne room.

As he walked, Cole spotted overgrown animals of all types – goats, rabbits and even a pigeon – bustling through the palace with food, fabrics and firewood. A few stopped in their tracks to look at Cole in interest; others averted their gaze. All of them were dressed in fine palace livery.

"Where am I? What is this place?" Cole asked, staring at the pillars, intricate tiles and vaulted roof. The ceiling was decorated with swirling stars and planets that glittered with gold leaf. Unable to bear the silence that followed his question, he added, "Th-this is a lovely palace. Definitely the nicest thing I've seen today."

The wolf said nothing but continued to walk purposefully across the throne room. It was a large, open space with a raised dais at one end and an attached courtyard barely visible on the other side. An ornate, upholstered chair sat proudly in the centre of the stage.

"That's not to say that you're not lovely," Cole rambled on. "You are a lovely wolf, aren't you?" Then, it occurred to him that the intelligent, sharp-toothed creature might not like being talked to like the miniature poodle that lived down the end of his street, and he stopped talking.

Along the corridor from the throne room stood a pair of heavy doors. Some kind of tree was intricately carved upon them and they looked old but well polished. The wolf approached and rapped three times on the wood. A thin echo bounced down the hallway and, from beyond the door, footfalls approached.

"What's through there?" asked Cole.

The wolf ignored his question. "You talk too much, elseworlder."

Elseworlder? Cole gulped and clamped his mouth shut. He waited, listening to the footsteps growing louder and bracing himself for something to appear that was even stranger than badgers in clothes. With a soft creak, the double doors opened.

The man who glided into view looked human. He had a pointed white beard and a red velvet waistcoat, and was very tall. He held his hands out to Cole in welcome.

"Introductions!" said the man with a kind smile. "I am King Enk. This is my kingdom and you," he added with a flash of his dark eyes, "you are the one we have been waiting for, Cole."

CHAPTER THREE
THE MAGICAL TEOQUAT FRUIT

The king's study was like nothing Cole had ever seen before. The walls were of veined marble and the ceiling was painted gold. In a vast hearth, a fire danced in flames of purple, turquoise and orange; warm, insect-like specks of light fluttered overhead.

"Please, make yourself at home," said the king as they stepped into the room.

Cole didn't know what to look at first. If he had thought that Grandma Jenny's house was old-fashioned, this place was something else. The room was lit by flaming torches in wall brackets. Empty suits of armour stood sentry behind the doors and the startling quiet alerted Cole to the fact that he had not seen or heard anything that was powered by electricity in any of the palace's rooms or corridors. Ancient books, ornaments and scrolls were piled on shelves and rich paintings hung on the walls – *this* was a room of treasures.

"This place feels alive," Cole breathed, leaning close to a tapestry of a luscious forest edging a lake with water like white crystal. "The pictures keep moving!" He could almost feel the wind in the trees and the icy cold beneath the water's surface.

"I wouldn't get too close – you might get lost in there," warned the king as he settled himself into a chair and lit a pipe.

Cole glanced over. The man's face shimmered with reflected light from the fire, like the porcelain plates that Grandma Jenny kept on her dresser in the kitchen. His eyes were acorn-shaped and shining like marbles. When he sat, Cole could see his whole body, which was long and gangly with twisted joints, making him look like he was made of splintered wood.

"What is all this stuff?" Cole asked, gazing around the room. On a high shelf, a glass ball spun by itself. A strange, white mask hummed faintly. A mobile of stars and symbols tinkled and chimed.

"I'm a collector of magical artefacts: jewellery, trinkets

and machines of every kind," the king explained.

"Like Grandma Jenny with her attic," Cole mused.

The king smiled. "Some of my treasures are from lands beyond the mountains and over the sea. Most are local to our world, Deriuss."

"Your world?" Cole had suspected, since arriving through the mousehole, that he was no longer in his own world – talking animals and magic clouds were definitely not covered in his lessons on science or world geography – but it was nice to hear someone confirm it.

"The world of Deriuss, yes. Of course, I send explorers to all the elsewheres looking for wonders."

At the mention of explorers raiding worlds for treasures, Cole's finger throbbed. He recalled the image of the knee-high mouse, and flashed with annoyance at the little terror thinking that it could just come into Grandma Jenny's house and steal whatever it wanted. Cole was about to tell the king as much when he swiftly moved the conversation on.

"Actually, I have a marvellous device from your own world. Just there." The king pointed to a large plastic box with a lid. Cole lifted the lid to see an old-fashioned record player.

"My grandma has a record player like this." Cole flicked the switch on the side of the casing, but nothing happened.

"Your grandmother must be a powerful magician," said the king, reclining on the settee with his hands resting on his belly.

Cole placed the tiny needle onto the record as he'd seen Grandma Jenny do, expecting drums to rattle or a crescendo to fill the room. To his disappointment, the record remained still and silent. Realising the problem, Cole chuckled.

"Not really," he said. "It's just electricity." He perched on an empty settee opposite the king.

"These treasures come from all regions," King Enk told him. "Felrin in the valley, Narwan beyond the hills or right here, in the city of Alfar."

"Alfar," Cole repeated, chewing over the word. "That's the city I saw inside the walls?"

King Enk nodded. "It surrounds the palace. It is the jewel of my kingdom. The land of Deriuss stretches as far as the eye can see and beyond, and for as long as there has been water in its rivers, clouds in its sky and mystery in its heart, I have been its guardian."

Cole thought of the mirage of green that he had seen when he had walked through the gates of the city. There had been streams of crystal-clear water, low-hanging trees blooming with fruits and flowers that created a thick, heady perfume – but the vast, parched world beyond the walls could not have been more different.

"I didn't see any rivers or clouds outside the city," Cole mused, and then hastily added, "I like this place, though. It's incredible!"

A sad smile filled the king's face. "You are not the first to say so. As for the rest of the world, that is where you can help us."

The king gave a swish of his hand and the fire in the hearth turned a beautiful shade of magenta. The flames licked higher beside the pair, and Cole was wrapped in a gentle warmth. The journey to the palace had left him grimy and dirty, yet now, he felt clean and his clothes smelled of lavender, as if freshly washed.

Cole's heart started to beat quickly. "How did you do that? Is it magic? Real magic, not just a trick?"

The king chuckled. "For Derians, it is the spirit of the world. It is the power that we use for food, light and warmth, and I alone am its master. Would you like to see some more?"

"Oh, yes, please!" said Cole, leaning forward eagerly. "I've always wanted to do magic. I know some card tricks but they're not really magic, are they? I've always wished I could do things like turning someone into a slug or making it snow or whipping up a plate of pancakes out of thin air –"

Cole stopped himself at the sight of the amused expression on King Enk's face. "Sorry," he mumbled. "I've been told that I talk too much."

The king chuckled. "A feast would be just what we need, don't you think?" He closed his eyes and reposed in his chair for a few seconds, Cole watching him intently. When he opened his eyes, Cole followed his gaze and jumped with surprise as silver, jewel-encrusted platters lay on the table in front of him, bursting with decadent delicacies.

"Dig in," said the king.

Cole tucked into the food with his fingers, not sparing a thought for plates or napkins or cutlery. There were savoury pastries shaped like birds and sweet pastries shaped like flowers. "This is delicious," said Cole as crumbs rained from his mouth. There were sugar-sweet fruits scooped into colourful balls. "So amazing," sighed Cole as juice dribbled down his chin. After that, there was ice cream and fairy cakes and a bowl of rich, brown goo which turned out to be the most incredible chocolate mousse Cole had ever tasted. "This is my new favourite food," he declared, running his finger around the nearly empty bowl.

The king took a lilac cupcake and ate it in one swallow. "So now, you see some of the power that the land of Deriuss holds."

Cole collapsed onto the sofa cushions, his stomach bulging. Somehow, the empty platters had already disappeared from the table and the crumbs and chocolate stains had vanished from Cole's clothes.

The king had stood up. "You are a special boy, Cole. Very special indeed." He stroked his beard thoughtfully for a moment before running a thin hand around the edge of the record player that Cole had played with. "You know much about these artefacts of mine and you show great spirit."

Cole felt his face flush pink. "I'm nothing special," he said, and he sank deeper into the cushions. He grew tired and wondered fuzzily if it was against the law to nap on the king's settee. "I only came to Deriuss because that mouse stole my grandma's brooch and I wanted to get it back."

As he said the words, he looked down at his right hand. Inexplicably, he had pulled the shining, circular object out of his pocket without realising and was stroking it gently with his thumb. The lights dancing above his head were reflected in the shimmering jewels and he again felt a different sensation as he passed his fingers over each one.

"The seal of Felrin," said the king gently. "It never belonged to your grandma, Cole. It is an ancient Derian artefact. It controls the magic in our land and this one has been lost for many decades now. Your touch was the magical charge needed to draw my agent to you, like a moth to a flame."

The king began to walk towards the door of the chamber and, listening hard, Cole was vaguely aware that he was standing up and following him. "Where are we going?" he asked, taking control of his legs and running to keep up with the king's stride.

"You need to understand why the seal of Felrin is important to the people of Deriuss," said the old king, "and why it is essential that it remains in my palace."

They walked along the corridor and back out into the

vast throne room with its tall windows and polished dais. Crossing it, they stepped out into an internal courtyard, lined with white stone arches and filled – crammed – with twisted, gnarled fruit trees. Vines crept along the thick palace walls in every direction and their leaves swished from left to right almost as if they were breathing. Sunlight streamed into the small, paved square and landed on the most spectacular centrepiece.

It was something like a fountain or water feature that might have been found in the gardens of a stately home. Fashioned from yet more gleaming marble, a large carved basin decorated with gold supported a tower of smaller bowls. Golden leaves, flowers and fruits of all kinds wound their way around each element of the exquisite fountain, which gleamed as though brand new. Around its base were a score of circular, gold seals, each one glistening with its own jewels. Among them, a singular empty indentation suggested that one seal was missing.

"This, Cole," said the king in a hushed voice, "is the source of our magic. The well here in Alfar is truly the lifeblood of the land of Deriuss. This magic is what makes the grass grow in the spring and the rain fall in the autumn. Without it, we could not live. Every citizen of Deriuss depends upon it."

Cole gazed at the magic well in frozen awe. From its depths,

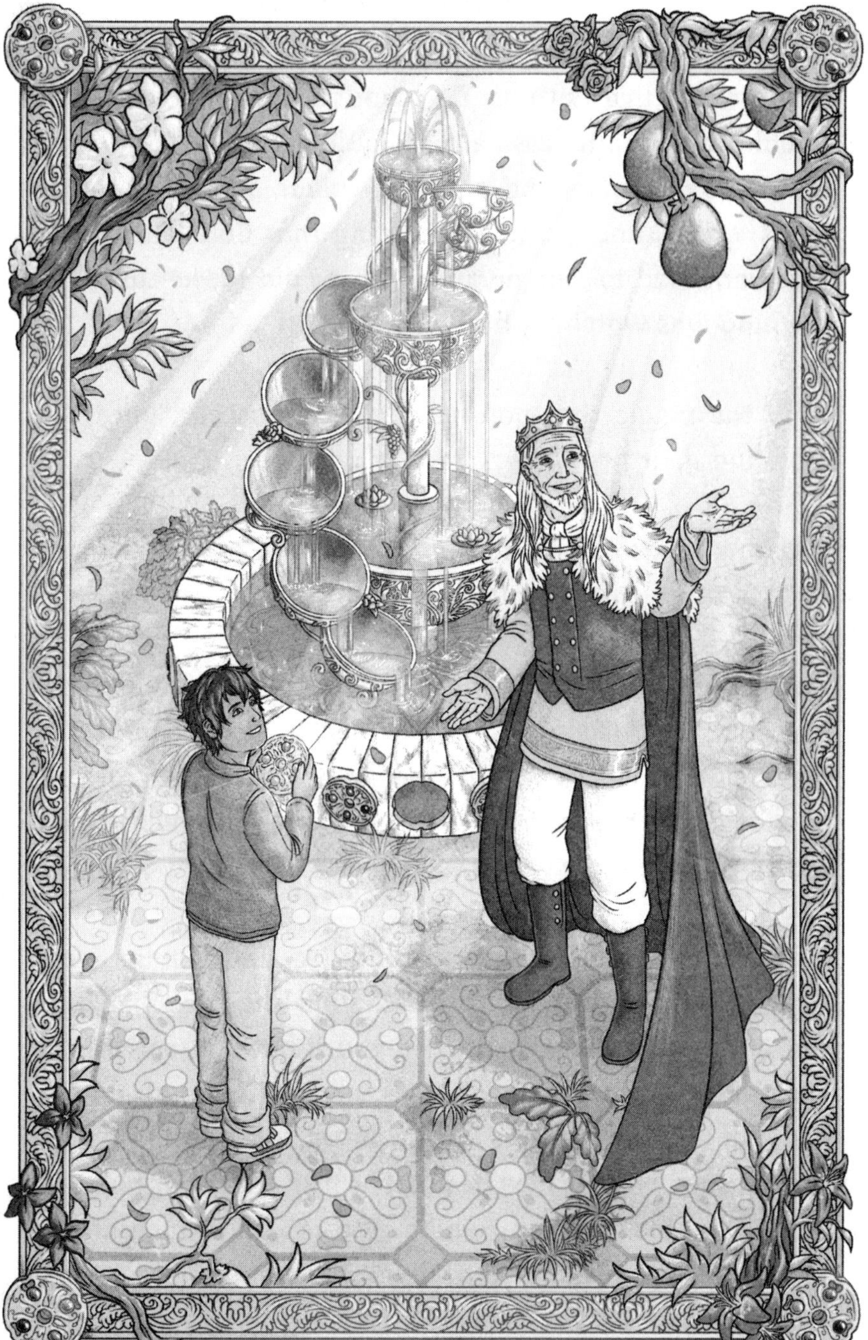

a substance like nothing Cole had ever seen pooled and bubbled merrily. It was neither liquid nor gas and, as Cole watched, it shifted and changed colour. It sped through blues, greens and purples so quickly that Cole felt a little dizzy and had to look away. When he did so, he saw that the king was watching him with interest.

"And the magic that you can do," Cole asked, "with the food and your fire –"

The king smiled. "Ah," he said. "That is a power afforded only to those who eat of the teoquat fruit."

Cole's bemusement must have shown on his face because the king chuckled softly. He nodded towards one of the trees to Cole's left. "These are teoquat trees. They are grown of magic and bear a fruit called the teoquat which, when eaten, has the most wondrous effects."

Cole examined the closest teoquat tree. The boughs were long and twisted; it looked as though the trees had run out of space to grow in the courtyard but had carried on regardless. Its knotted branches were so entangled with those of the trees around it that it was hard to tell where one finished and the next began. The fruit itself was bulbous and heavy-looking, somewhere between an orange and a pear. A strong smell oozed from its skin, not unpleasant but pungent enough to make Cole's eyes water. It seemed that this whole courtyard was buzzing with magical power.

"As you have seen," the king continued, "there are many parts of Deriuss that are not yet touched by the magic of the Alfarian well. These seals" – he gestured at the many circular ornaments lining the edge of the well – "are the key to expanding the reach of our magic and, now that you have returned the final seal to us, I can restore all of Deriuss to the prosperous land that it once was. With its return, we are complete. You have done the people of Deriuss a great kindness, Cole."

Cole looked up, and saw that the king was holding out his hand. He said no words, but Cole could hear the silent command.

A distant part of Cole was determined to tuck the seal back into his pocket and take it straight back to Grandma Jenny. On the other hand, the image of the barren wasteland beyond the city walls had been haunting him since he had first set foot in the king's palace. He had seen villages and towns in the valley – people were *living* in that heat. Before he could make up his mind, however, his hand had taken control and he had dropped the seal into the king's outstretched palm.

"Thank you," said the king, smiling.

Cole nodded. "I knew that it was special."

King Enk turned the seal of Felrin around his fingers and the jewels flashed. "I can offer you something as a reward," he said, tucking the seal back inside his waistcoat and out of sight. "I have seen something unique in you. I believe that you could be a great magician one day."

"Really?" Warmth grew throughout Cole's body and he suddenly felt taller, stronger and brighter. It had nothing to do with the delicious food or the sunlight raining down on the courtyard. The king thought that he was special! Visions danced in his head of him flying through the air casting spells while Liam and Mara looked on enviously. "Could I really learn to do magic like you can?"

"You could," said the king, and he raised a hand high into the air and snapped his fingers.

Out of the shadows of one of the arches lining the courtyard stepped the tall, white wolf who had delivered Cole to the palace. With a small bow to King Enk, she plucked a singular fruit free from the nearest branch with her razor-like claws.

"I've been looking for a new apprentice – someone just like you," said the king as the wolf stood between them holding the teoquat fruit on a small platter. "There is one condition, however."

"What condition?" said Cole, gazing at the fruit. "I don't mind hard work and I promise to always do my homework. I'll learn whatever spells you want."

"You're a good boy, Cole," said the king. With a delicate hand, he took the strange fruit off the platter and held it softly, as though it were made of crystal. "I have already explained that to use that particular kind of magic, you must first eat the fruit of the teoquat tree. I have consumed the fruit's magic for many years and I am now its master."

Cole stared at the fruit. It did not look like it would taste unpleasant – why, then, was the king looking so serious all of a sudden?

"It will be quite an event, I assure you," Enk continued, "but you see, this is a magical fruit. It is tied to this world and its magic can therefore only ever be used in Deriuss. The teoquat will reveal your true nature as well as your magical potential. Once you take this magic, you must stay in Deriuss – forever."

Cole swallowed. "Forever? But that's – I mean – *forever* forever?"

The king merely smiled and walked calmly around his courtyard before stopping to rest on a bench, where he sat patiently and watched a small bird hopping around on the ground.

Cole thought hard. At home, he had never been good at anything – not unless you counted talking the hind legs off a donkey, and most people thought that was a curse, not a skill. He could stay here, in Deriuss, and learn magic from a king! It was more than most children could dream of.

He took a seat next to the king and brought his hands up to his face to help him to think clearly. As he did so, the scent of his newly and magically laundered clothing filled his nose: lavender, the scent which reminded him most of his grandma. He thought of his mum and dad, of Liam and Mara and of Grandma Jenny's sparkling eyes. Could he really leave all that behind without even a goodbye, just to make magical desserts?

Cole sighed. "I'm sorry, but I have to go home. My family will miss me and I'll miss them."

The king smiled again, nodding sagely. "I understand your

decision. You must be true to your heart's desire. In that case, my captain, Serla, will organise a carriage for your safe return to the portal." The king snapped his fingers again and the white wolf, having disposed of the fruit, reappeared at his side. "The carriage will take you there directly. Oh, and Cole," he added as the wolf led Cole from the courtyard, "if you change your mind, you are always welcome."

*

King Enk's carriage was nearly as sumptuous as his study. Seats of dark green velvet cushioned Cole on the bumpy ride and thick curtains offered some protection from the stifling evening air. The oppressive heat had hit him all over as soon as he had left Alfar. Looking at the darkening, silent world around him, Cole couldn't find much in common with King Enk's description of Deriuss.

He was eager to get home. What if his parents had been looking for him? Still, as they sped through the sparse forest, Cole couldn't help but wonder: what would it be like to learn real magic? To live in a palace? To be the most brilliant magician of his age?

Cole was lost in a daydream when the carriage pulled to an abrupt stop. He jumped out and landed on the cracked ground. The grey horses that were pulling the carriage stamped and tossed their heads.

"Thank you for the ride. I very much enjoyed my trip into your world," he said to them, and waited for a reply. They simply huffed, just as horses did in his own world.

The wolf in the driver's seat flicked the reins. With a clatter of wheels, the carriage whirled away into the forest.

Cole peered through the gloom for the tree with the gap between its roots. He paced around the small clearing, thinking of magic, of lavender and the comforts of home. He rolled up his sleeves and was just wondering if the wolf had brought him to the right place when a voice burst out of the thicket of trees.

"*Get him!*"

CHAPTER FOUR
A KIDNAPPING

Cole was tossed up and down on the splintery wood and, with his hands and legs tied and a sack covering his head, it was all he could do not to slide about like spilled fruit. He was going to feel sore after this journey.

"We didn't need to tie him up."

"We did! What if he escaped?"

"Maybe if we'd just explained..."

"Explained?! Explained what?"

The kidnappers had not stopped bickering since they had captured Cole in the forest. He knew that there were at least two of them, one with a much higher voice than the other. They were now speeding through the forest on what felt like a rickety wagon.

The higher voice continued. "If someone came up to you and said, 'Excuse me, but I just need to kidnap you for a bit, do you mind?', what would you say?"

"I wouldn't say anything. I'd run," replied the lower voice.

"Exactly! And then we'd be no closer to the seal."

Cole grunted as the wagon bounced over a jagged rock, throwing him up in the air. With his back sore and his head throbbing, Cole tried to make sense of what he was hearing. They were after the seal of Felrin! But Cole had entrusted it to the king so that it could be kept safe in his marble palace on the mountaintop, where it belonged. Should he tell his kidnappers?

"Careful how you go, Piog. We need the elseworlder alive."

"You keep distracting me," he complained.

"I could take over if you like."

"I'm fine, Meeka! Stop telling me what to do."

Cole's mind was racing. If he told them that he didn't have the seal, they might let him go. But what if they did something nasty to him instead? He shuddered. It wasn't worth the risk.

"Hey! Elseworlder!" called the sharp voice. "You in one piece?"

Cole froze. He clamped his lips shut underneath the hessian sack. He couldn't let his big mouth get him into any more trouble.

"I'm talking to you." They reached over and shook his arm. Cole forced his body to fall floppy. "Out cold."

"Typical!" groaned the voice named Piog. "*Now* how will he tell us what we need? We might have to dunk him in the fire pits until he wakes up."

They *were* going to torture him, whether he had the seal or not. Cole had to escape, and quickly. He lay still for a moment, waiting. As the pair began to bicker about which route to take through the forest, Cole formulated a plan.

A dry breeze blew through the weave of the sack, so he was quite certain that the wagon was uncovered. He could simply throw himself over the side, but the kidnappers would be on him in seconds. Slowly, he inched up against the wall of the wagon and felt along the side until he found a jagged nail sticking out of the wall. Easing his hands closer, he began to scrape his bindings up and down against the nail, loosening the rope.

Cole was careful to time his scraping so that it was covered by their conversation. After missing the turning for the shortcut and the argument that followed, the pair moved onto the topic of food.

"I'd love some fish stew for dinner," Piog mused.

"You'll be lucky. It'll be hot grains and a bite of black bread, like always."

"I bet Mum could make a great fish stew. With proper vegetables – green ones, I mean..."

"You don't even know if you like fish."

"...and potato salad with spring onions..."

"How do *you* know what spring onions taste like?"

"...fresh peas with butter melting on top and a sprig of mint..."

With his kidnappers distracted, it was easy to pick apart the rope with the rusty nail. With a final sharp tug, Cole's wrists were free and he slid the sack off his head, but the glare of the maple-coloured sunset forced him to blink rapidly. Cole looked up just in time to see that the forest had given way to a town of low, thatched buildings with candles glowing in the windows. The streets were almost deserted but for a few people wandering aimlessly.

"Here we are," Piog said, pulling up next to a decrepit, timber-framed cottage.

In spite of his bound ankles, Cole grabbed the side of the wagon and swung himself over. He landed with a thud onto the cobbled street, but there wasn't time to waste. He pulled himself upright and hopped away towards the line of trees at the edge of the town.

"Hey!" one of the kidnappers called.

"Come back here," said the other, thundering after him.

"Get off me!" Cole protested as two pairs of arms grabbed him. He kicked and elbowed and was almost free when orange light spilled across the darkening street.

"What *are* you doing?!" yelled a silhouette from the doorway of the small cottage.

The girl named Meeka groaned. "Uh-oh."

"I didn't raise my children to behave like hooligans!" yelled the silhouette, who turned out to be a stout woman with a rolling pin held menacingly in her hand.

"But, Mum, it's for a good cause..." protested Meeka.

Cole looked up at the woman who was glowing in the light from the cottage windows. She was surprisingly short and stocky with very short hair and olive skin. Her face was flushed and her grey eyes were scrunched with determination.

"...it's for the Resistance," Meeka continued, her voice trailing off nervously.

The woman in the doorway threw up her hands. "How many times have I told you not to get yourselves involved with that lot?"

Cole made an unsteady effort to rise to his feet but, with his ankles tied, he couldn't find his balance on the uneven ground and fell over.

"Here," Piog said, untying the rope and holding out a hand to Cole.

"Mum, you're not listening," pleaded Meeka. "He's got the seal of Felrin! Redbush saw him with it in the city. We wanted to –"

"Redbush?! I've told you about that troublesome creature." The woman then turned to Cole and gave him a long, measured stare.

He had to tell them.

"I – I don't have it," he garbled. "I gave it to King Enk." His stomach flipped. For the first time, he wondered whether or not he had done the right thing.

"You did *what*?" cried Meeka, in despair.

"Enough!" shouted the woman. "Come inside. Meeka will unload the cart and brush down the pony, and Piog will cook us some dinner before we all starve to death."

"Fish stew?" said Piog hopefully.

"Grains and black bread, as usual. You know that, Piog. There hasn't been anything else to eat since –"

"Yeah," said Piog, with a reproachful glance at Cole, "I know." He ducked to follow his mother gloomily through the low doorway into the cottage beyond and Cole, with a little jolt of unease at being invited into a strange house, did the same.

The inside of the cottage glowed with bright colours. Patterned cloth hung from every wall in shades of orange, yellow, pink and brown, giving Cole a surge of warmth and comfort in his weary body. A corner of the cottage was marked by an ancient loom, where a half-complete tapestry showing a blossoming tree sat silent. Shelves and niches were crammed with jostling clay jugs and figures. Low beams crossed the room, hung with herbs and strange implements. At one end, sacks of grain were nestled beside a second loom which held a half-finished rug. At the other end was a low bed covered in a thin, brightly-coloured blanket. There were no other rooms, so Cole guessed that this was their kitchen, living room and bedroom all in one. Though it was small, the orange fire roaring in the hearth made the place wonderfully cosy.

"I am Yognar, and you are most welcome in Felrin," said the woman, bustling into the cottage and poking the fire. "What shall we call you?"

"This is Felrin?" asked Cole quickly, recognising the name. "Oh, I mean – I'm Cole," he said, then cursed himself for telling the truth. These people had just kidnapped him, after all. However, he had no way of knowing the way back to the portal from here – wherever 'here' was – and something about these new acquaintances fascinated Cole, so he abandoned any remaining urges to run away and took a few more steps into the middle of the room.

"Nice to meet you, Cole," Yognar was saying. "That pair are my twins, Piog and Meeka, and they are going to be in a lot of trouble for what they did to you."

"But, Mum...!" Piog moaned as Meeka reappeared from brushing the pony.

"But nothing! You carry on with that dinner and I'll not hear another word about it."

Yognar led Cole to the fire and sat him on a colourful rug of orange and pink triangles. All around the small cottage were blankets, needlework pictures and detailed tapestries showing images of great battles. In fact, they were identical to the style Cole had seen in King Enk's palace. Each picture had the strange look of being three-dimensional, as though it would be easy to step through the fabric into the world beyond.

Yognar caught him looking. "I make them for the king and the people in the capital. My mother taught me how, as did her mother before her."

"They're wonderful," Cole said truthfully.

"They're the only reason we eat," she replied, and Cole knew that the conversation was over.

Piog knelt by the fire to pour grains and water into a great iron pot like a cauldron. He reached up to grab leaves and garlic cloves from the beams and tossed them in. Soon, a rich, savoury smell filled the smoky air in the cottage.

"There, now. We'll soon get you fed and back to your own world," said Yognar.

"You'll really take me home?" asked Cole.

"You don't belong here. What the twins were thinking, I don't know..."

"It was Meeka's idea, Mum," Piog protested, stirring the cauldron of beige slop with an enormous ladle.

"But you went along with it, Piog. You could have said no," said Yognar reprovingly, now fetching bowls carved from golden wood. She handed Cole a bowl filled with steaming grains and a chunk of bread. It might have been like lumpy porridge, or perhaps sticky rice, except that it tasted of very little except for garlic, and the bread was solid and black.

Cole hadn't realised how hungry he was. He had eaten plenty of magical cakes and treats at the king's palace and ought to be full to bursting – yet he felt empty and hollow inside. Now, however, the more he ate, the more he felt like his old self. He didn't know why, but Cole liked this place, and he trusted Yognar. She was brisk and cross but seemed to genuinely care. The food was chewy and stale and as far away from the king's sugary feast as possible, but at least it was real.

"There," said Yognar. "What better way to make friends than over a meal?"

Piog and Meeka joined Cole and Yognar beside the fire and began to eat greedily, chatting between mouthfuls. Meeka looked at Cole with a furrowed brow. "You like it?"

"Delicious," Cole said. It was almost true, especially if he compared the mushy grains to the feeling of an empty stomach.

Piog raised an eyebrow. "If you think this is delicious, food must be disgusting in your world."

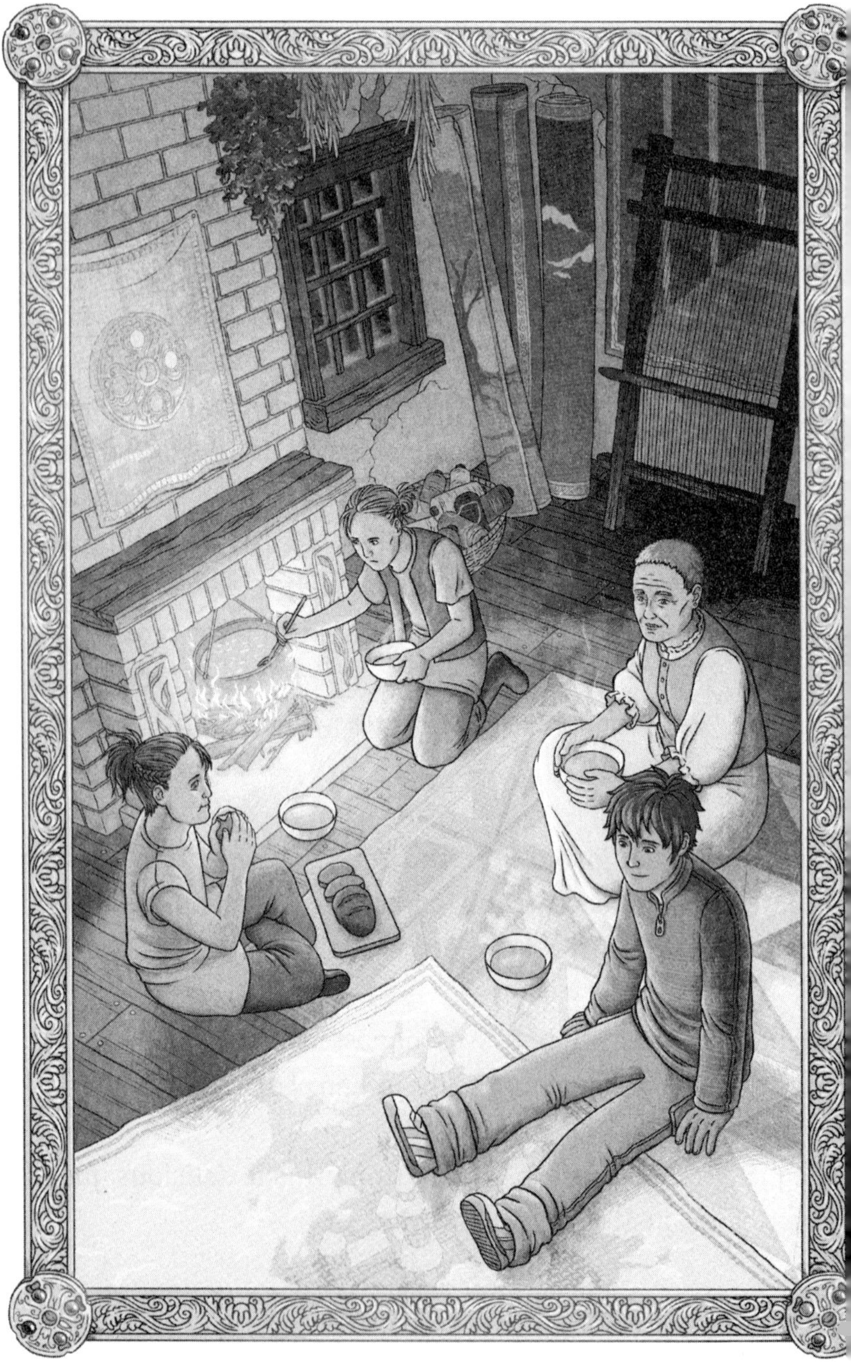

"It's all we've got," said Yognar apologetically, putting down her empty bowl with a sigh. "So, we make do."

"But why should we, Mum?" said Meeka, in a voice which suggested that she had asked this question many times before.

"Because no one has enough to eat," replied Yognar, similarly dully.

"In Alfar, they have everything they could ever eat. Fish stew and fresh peas and cakes and pastries."

"We don't know that, Meeka."

"Actually," Cole interrupted, "they *do* have cakes and pastries. The most delicious, light, creamy cakes and pastries in the world."

"See!" Meeka cried. "I told you."

Yognar looked lost for words, so Cole did what he did best and filled the silence. "Yeah, the king magicked it all out of thin air. He told me that, with the seal that I gave him, he could return to you all the magic that you need. So that's good, isn't it? You'll have rain and things will grow again."

There was a short pause, during which the twins exchanged thunderous glances and Yognar looked hard at Cole. "What do you mean, 'out of thin air'?"

Nonplussed, Cole replied, "I mean, one second there was an empty table and the next, it was full of plates of food. Why? Isn't that normal here?"

Yognar was breathing heavily. "That's not natural. What exactly did Enk tell you the seal of Felrin was for?"

Cole swallowed. "Uh, well, there was this magic fountain in his palace and all the seals were designed to fit into it and he said that they helped the magic to flow into the land..." He trailed off at the sight of the looks on the three faces around the fire.

"The king has always kept all the magic in Deriuss for himself," sneered Piog. "He's scared that if he let places like Felrin have their magic back, the people would rise up against him."

"Well, he's right. We would," said Meeka.

"But why?" asked Cole.

Gathering the empty bowls, Yognar said, "In Deriuss, the

turning of the seasons, the flowing of rivers, the growing of crops – they're all tied to the magic of the land. Once, long ago, magic simply infused the soil, flowing freely wherever it wanted to go. Wherever the magic went, the people of Deriuss followed, living off the plants and animals that they found in each place and relying on the repeating pattern of the seasons."

Cole thought of the seal and the four coloured jewels around it. He remembered the feeling of springtime warmth caused by the green jewel as well as the hunger and cold that came from the blue. He looked up at Yognar, his face a reflection of thought, and she continued as she poked the fire again.

"In time, the population grew, and the people became tired of moving from valley to peak to plain. So, they found a way to collect pools of magic in each city and settlement – a bit like building a dam to turn a river into a lake – and each magic pool is operated by an ancient seal."

Cole was confused. "You mean, there's a magic pool here in Felrin?"

She nodded sadly. "In a manner of speaking. Hundreds of years ago, King Enk was crowned and became infatuated with owning all the magic in the land. He started to collect the seals."

"Wait," interrupted Cole. "You said *hundreds of years ago.* But I saw the king today – he's not that old."

Piog gave a derisive snort of laughter. "He's at least three hundred years old."

Cole stared at Piog. "What?!"

Yognar sighed. "No one alive can remember it, but it is said that the king became power-hungry and began to collect the seals from the well of every town in the land. He forced his servants to build him a huge well in his palace and, with every new seal that he added, the magic in Alfar grew stronger and all the magical wells around the land began to dry up."

"History says that the pools didn't dry up all at once so, for years, we still had the seasons and our ancestors could still grow a little for themselves. Now, though, the well is dry. We can't grow anything for ourselves but we get rations" – she glanced at the grains in the corner of the room – "from the capital. Poor Meeka and Piog have never known it any other way." Yognar stood up wearily and began to make tea in a small clay teapot.

Piog piped up. "I felt rain, once," he told his mother proudly. "On a trip to the palace. A cloud burst right over my head!" To his right, Meeka scowled enviously.

Cole's stomach had turned to lead. He thought guiltily of the magic that he had wasted on a load of cakes which hadn't even filled him up, when here were Yognar, Piog, Meeka and the rest of the Derians, scraping by with tasteless beans and gritty bread. He considered the little that he had seen of the land outside the palace, remembering the dry, dusty ground, the dirt washed onto his clothes and then the feeling of relief when he had walked into King Enk's palace. It seemed as though all the joy, life and beauty in Deriuss was kept there.

"So, the seals don't belong in Alfar?" he asked, tentatively.

"No," said Meeka, perhaps a little louder than she had intended. "The seal of Felrin belongs here, in our magic well."

"That's the seal that I found in my grandma's attic," said Cole weakly, as Yognar handed him a mug of hot water infused with leaves. "How did it get there?"

Meeka answered. "They say that, when the king started to get greedy, some settlements hid their seals away so that he would never find them. Perhaps they were planning to recover them once he was gone, but no one expected him to live such a long time – we're not sure how he does it."

"Never mind that," said Yognar, looking concerned. "I'm more worried about this 'out of thin air' magic. The seals can unlock the magic of the land, but I've never heard of it allowing someone to make things appear from nowhere. What did it look like, Cole?"

Cole described what had occurred in the king's chambers and, as he cradled his warm mug and let his mind absorb all this new information, something that the king had told him slipped into his thoughts.

"These are teoquat trees. They are grown of magic and bear a fruit called the teoquat which, when eaten, has the most wondrous effects."

When he relayed this to the small group, Meeka stood up at once. "That's how he's doing it! He's found some tree that gives him magical powers! We've got to get our hands on that fruit!"

Yognar pulled Meeka back down onto her seat. "No, we do not," she said firmly. "From what Cole has described, these trees sound like a mutation of the magic that has been cooped up and condensed with no room to grow. It's not natural and those trees should be treated with great caution. If the king has been living off the fruit, I bet that all the natural energy stored in that well has been keeping him alive."

There was a short silence. The impact of everything that had been said seemed to hang in the air.

"Someone's got to tell the Resistance," Piog stated finally.

"I won't hear another word," Yognar announced. "Poor Cole must be worn out. Now, Cole, I'll make up a bed for you in front of the fire. The privy is a little shed round the back. Piog and Meeka will take you back up to the forest at first light, so that you can go home."

Cole nodded and yawned. He had not told the twins or Yognar that the king had offered him the chance to eat the teoquat fruit. Why would a king so obsessed with power choose to share it with a – what did they call it? – an 'elseworlder'? He had called Cole 'special'...

Cole dragged himself into the pile of rugs that Yognar had heaped beside the hearth. He thought that his family would know for sure that he was missing and must be looking for him, but he did feel exhausted and it must be late. As the family got comfortable in the bed by the wall, he closed his eyes, the image of King Enk, his lavish palace and the heady scent of the teoquat fruit dancing through his mind.

CHAPTER FIVE
THE EMPTY WELL

Cole was awoken by a clanging bell. Surely, it wasn't time for school yet. His sleep-filled mind was shaking off images from the strangest dream: kings, magic, talking wolves and kidnap.

It took him a moment to remember where he was. The fire in the hearth had died down to embers but smoke lingered in the air. As Cole threw off the colourful rugs that were piled on top of him, he was hit by the hot morning air.

Cole's Derian hosts grumbled as they wriggled out of their bed covers and pulled on their day clothes. "G'morning, Cole," Yognar murmured.

"Uh, hi," Cole replied, still not quite sure that this was, in fact, real. The bell was still ringing; it sounded like it was coming from somewhere a few streets away.

"Kids, Enk's envoys are on their way," Yognar explained, pulling on straw sandals. "We have to go to the town square to hear the message. Here, Cole, put this on... and these... and wrap this around you. They should keep you hidden."

"Hidden?" Cole asked, confused.

"Absolutely, hidden," she replied. "King Enk sent you back to the portal. If he or any of his servants see that you're still here, he'll want to know why."

"Mum's right," yawned Piog. "Who in their right mind would choose this place over Alfar? It's very suspicious."

Wearing old boots that were too big, a straw hat and a thick, orange rug that Yognar tied around his shoulders like a cloak, Cole set out with her and the twins into the middle of the town. As they traipsed blearily down the shabby street, the morning sun beat down on them, staining the cobblestones orange-pink. It was strangely quiet – no wind blew and no birds sang, and Cole was starting to see what having no seasons must mean for the people of Felrin. Members of the town were stumbling out of doorways and shuffling what must have been a familiar route towards the central square, as a metal bell rang from the top of a short tower.

After his long rest, Cole was feeling extremely talkative. "How big is Felrin? It looks bigger than the town I live in. Are there many other cities in Deriuss, besides here and Alfar? I saw a talking mouse and a wolf yesterday – can your pony talk, too? And is it always this *hot*?"

The twins took it in turns to grunt answers. Alfar was the biggest city in Deriuss; yes, there were others, but to get to them you had to cross the mountains, which was very difficult in these conditions; no, not all animals in Deriuss could talk, but you could usually tell which ones could because they wore clothes; the lack of seasons meant that, yes, the weather was always the same.

Cole gazed in awe at the higgledy-piggledy buildings and paddocks, the donkeys and mules pulling wagons and the shop fronts selling chipped crockery and faded fabrics. Beaten pathways led through the town towards a collection of taller buildings in the distance, where the streets opened up into the square. Though the buildings here were grander in stature, they were still rickety-looking and a little lopsided, as if they hadn't been properly looked after in a long time. In the centre of the square was a large, stone basin with a plinth rising from the centre. It looked like a dried-up fountain.

"Is that…"

"Yeah," said Piog. "That's our *magic well.*" There was a good deal of sullen sarcasm in his voice. "The seal of Felrin is meant to fit into that empty circle, there."

Cole peered closer. On the side of the well was a circle of smooth stone, as if a section had been cut out from the rock.

"Can we go and look?" asked Cole, but by then, the jostling crowd was too big. The four of them were pushed and shoved towards one side of the square, overshadowed by a huge building.

Some of the building's windows were boarded up and the flags that fluttered from the poles were drab and bleached by the sun, but Cole could tell that it had once been very impressive. The crowd faced the stone steps expectantly. Although it was still early morning, Cole noticed that many of the citizens of the town were fanning themselves with branches or folded pieces of parchment. Their faces were weathered, tanned and looked older than they should. One thing that stood out most of all was the absence of the animal folk from the palace – these people were all humans.

Soon, the doors of the building swung open and out marched a group of official-looking people in palace livery. Underneath, each was dressed in rich velvet in jewel-bright colours, so it was obvious that they were from prosperous Alfar. They were flanked by armoured wolves, who snarled at the crowd until the Derians fell quiet. Among them was the wolf named Serla, easily distinguishable by the grey streaks across her nose and her red cape.

A tall woman with a hollow-sounding voice stepped forwards, unfurling a scroll. "Hear ye, hear ye. The king commands you to be silent, to hear the following proclamation." She paused and waited for silence. "The seal of Felrin has been returned to us by an elseworlder."

Hushed murmurs broke out in the crowd. Many eyes darted in the direction of the stone basin in the centre of the square, which sat dry, dusty and cracked.

There was another pause, during which the woman scanned the crowd to gauge its reaction. Then, she said, "King Enk has decided that the final Derian seal shall remain in the palace. Its magic, under the guidance of our wise king, shall preserve the future of our land for all time."

Some seemed delighted that the seal had been found but most were furious that the king was keeping it in his palace instead of restoring it to Felrin's magic well. Cole was beginning to sweat under his hot disguise.

"That utter fool," grumbled a nearby voice.

"As you may or may not be aware, the seal of Felrin is the final seal needed to complete our king's noble work to unite the powers of this land in perfect harmony," the willowy woman continued over the murmuring from the crowd. "It is with great anticipation that we have awaited the return of the seal of Felrin to its rightful place in the palace."

The same voice beside Cole cursed once more. "That seal's rightful place is here. Doesn't Enk see that he's destroying his own kingdom?"

Cole looked round to see a figure dressed in a dark cloak. Cole stared at it, but its face was obscured by the darkness under a heavy hood. Shorter than most of the crowd, the figure was easy to miss, but Cole thought that there was something secretive in the way that it held its cloak over its bowed head.

"Psst, Redbush," Meeka hissed in the direction of the stranger. When it lifted its head slightly to shoot her a sideways glance, Cole saw long, delicate whiskers and dark red fur framing two large, black eyes. Still not used to

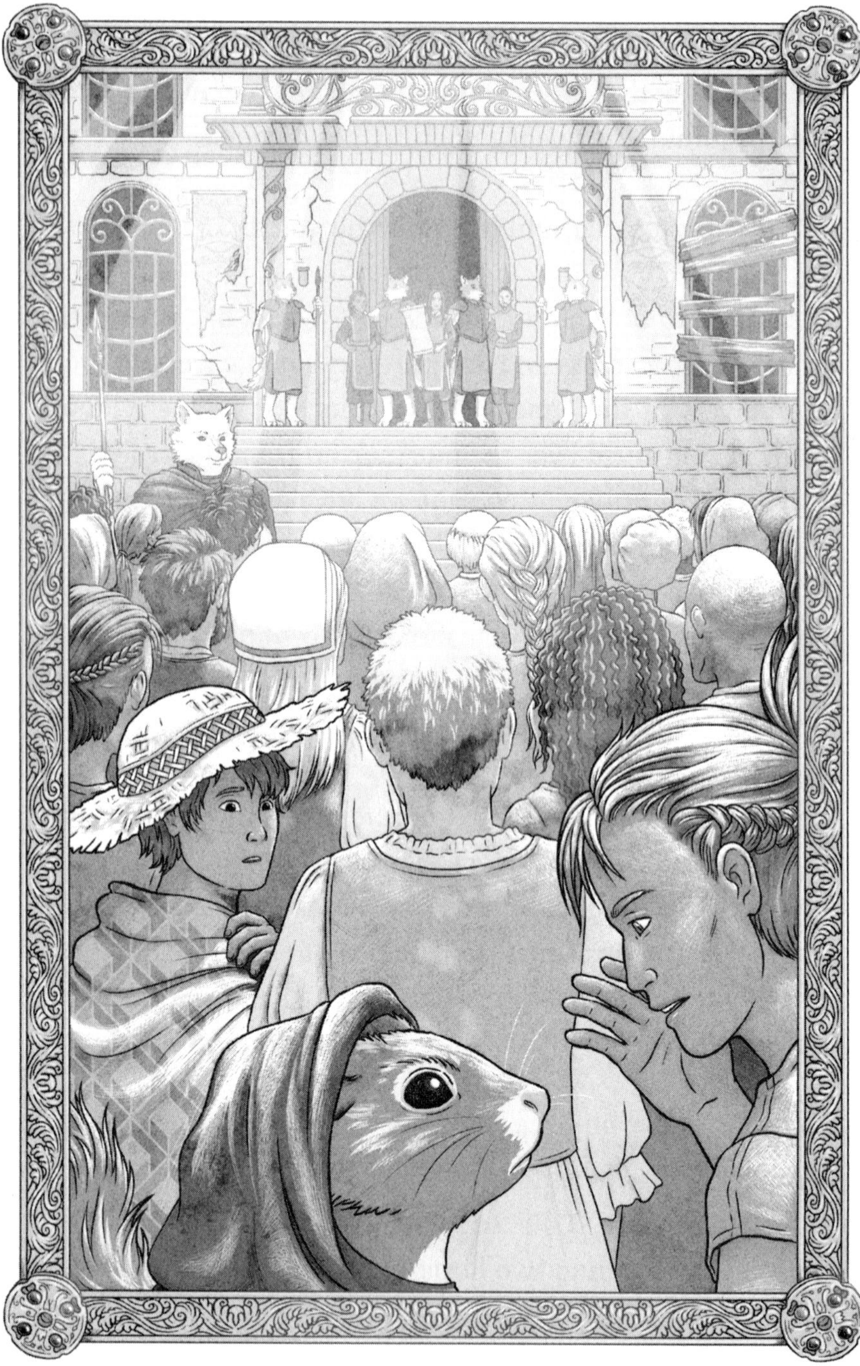

seeing overgrown animals wearing clothes, Cole scanned the crowd but all he saw were people like Yognar and the twins. While the palace had been full of animals behaving like humans, he had seen none outside of the city of Alfar besides this squirrel. Cole wondered why it was lurking so cautiously among the crowd.

"Is there going to be a meeting tonight?" Meeka was whispering.

Redbush nodded. "Absolutely," he said in an undertone. Carefully, he leaned this way and that to avoid the gaze of the large white wolf, who seemed to be scouring the square with her amber eyes. "I've been putting feelers out for a while. I've got people interested from Felrin, Putkip and even Narwan. They'll all be here tonight. This is too good an opportunity to miss."

"We'll be there," said Meeka, her expression burning with defiance.

"Shhh!" said Piog, with a glance towards Yognar. Redbush winked and backed into the crowd.

"Who was that?" asked Cole.

"Redbush," Piog muttered. "He's a fighter, like us."

On the steps, the wolves were stalking up and down, growling to bring the crowd to order. The lady continued. "In his infinite majesty and wisdom, King Enk has decreed that the citizens of Felrin will be permitted to celebrate in their own homes in honour of the seal's return. There will be a ball and a banquet for the citizens of Alfar, and a small shipment of food shall be supplied for the Derians to celebrate. During the celebrations, King Enk himself will bring together the seal of Felrin and its fellows" – she paused for effect, her chest heaving with self-importance – "and the prosperous future of Deriuss will be secured."

A wave of uncertainty washed across the crowd. Cole picked up snippets of resigned agreement, barely contained fury and question upon question from little ones. With the crowd subdued, the envoy and the rest of the entourage swept into a waiting carriage. The wolves bounded alongside as four gleaming horses trotted from the square in the direction of the looming mountain city of Alfar.

As the Derians tramped from the square, Meeka couldn't contain herself. "I hate him, I hate him! He's just rubbing it in. That seal belongs to *us*."

Piog nodded and Yognar sighed. "It hardly changes things, Meeka," said Yognar wearily. "We didn't have the seal

70

before and we don't have it now."

"But Mum, now he has them *all*! Plus, now we have a chance of getting it back."

Yognar stopped dead. "Don't you dare, my girl. I'm warning you – no more foolish schemes. I don't want the Resistance bringing you home from the palace in pieces, you hear me?"

Meeka grumbled but said nothing more.

"Now, it's high time you two got Cole back to his portal, and then you've got to make the latest delivery to the palace. Got it?"

*

Cole's second wagon ride with Piog and Meeka was a lot more comfortable than his first. Instead of being thrown in the back with boxes filled with tapestries and patchwork for Alfar, he sat at the front between the twins as they trotted through the streets of Felrin. The unsure roads were packed with dried earth, and brittle leaves swirled underfoot. There were ramshackle houses leaning shoulder to shoulder as if using their immediate neighbour for support. Cole thought how, if one were to give up and collapse, the whole town would fall like dominoes.

They followed the looping road out of town and up the steep mountainside. The sun's umber rays streaked through the tall, black trees; around them was plenty of space for fields and farms, if only something would grow.

"Do you go to the palace every day? Is this your job?" Cole had a million questions for Piog and Meeka and this was his last chance to ask them. He was beginning to feel sorry that he was leaving this extraordinary world so soon, but his family would be missing him. He'd been gone a whole day, after all.

"Our job is to take Mum's knitting and weaving to the palace. Then, they give us the town's rations. Everything would be so much easier if we had our own magic back in the well."

"What do you think will happen when the king puts all the seals together?" asked Cole.

Piog and Meeka exchanged dark looks. "Dunno," said Piog. "He's been trying to get hold of them all for as long as anyone can remember – it must be something really important if he's been looking for hundreds of years."

Meeka squeaked, "What if it makes him live forever?!"

"Shut up, Meeka," said Piog, but he looked uncertain. "No one can be immortal."

An uncomfortable silence passed between the three of them, where seconds felt like minutes and the journey to the portal seemed unending. Finally, Cole spoke. "So, is that what you'll be doing today? Delivering tapestries and blankets?"

The twins gave each other sideways glances.

"Sure," said Meeka. Then, she coughed. "Cole, you've been inside the palace, right? What's it like? We Derians don't get to go inside. They make us wait at the gate."

Cole told them everything he could remember, though it wasn't much: the grand gates, his afternoon tea with the king and the teoquat fruit.

"...and there's this big room in the middle with a ceiling like stars and doors all around it to different parts of the palace. It's unbelievably big. You could fit your cottage in it a hundred times over."

"That'll be where the ball is held," muttered Meeka to Piog.

"This room is straight from the front gates, right, Cole?"

"Yeah," said Cole, rubbing sweat from his face. "You just go up the steps, along a short corridor and... wait. Why do you want to know? What are you planning?"

"Nothing," said Piog, too quickly.

"You are, you're up to something. Is it to do with the Resistance? Yognar said it was dangerous –"

"Look!" Meeka exploded like a pot boiling over. "We're poor! We're hungry! Our lands are dying and it's all because of the King of Alfar. After all these years, the seal is back again. This is our chance to get back the magic that's rightfully ours; to return Felrin to the place we hear about in stories. We're going to meet with the Resistance today whether Mum likes it or not, and you can't stop us, elseworlder."

Cole sat for a moment, shaken by Meeka's passion.

"I won't stop you," he said. "It's not fair, what the king is doing. And I'm sorry about the seal. I should never have agreed to give it to him. I just had no idea what he was really like – I wish I had known."

"It wouldn't have helped," said Meeka miserably. "Enk is

too powerful."

A memory stirred in the back of Cole's mind. He remembered how his feet had walked him through the gates of Alfar and how his hands had acted of their own accord when he had handed over the seal. Perhaps Meeka was right and Cole had never really had a choice in the matter.

He chewed his lip. He thought about everything that had happened over the last day: about the city of Alfar, which burst with colour and light, and about the other Derians, who had nothing. He thought about how he had come into this world thinking that the seal was just a trinket belonging to Grandma Jenny and about how he, Cole, had unwittingly played a part in making the Derians' plight even worse.

"Turn around," Cole said suddenly.

"What?" said Piog, pulling the plodding pony to a halt.

"Grandma Jenny sent me to the attic to clean up a mess, and that's what I'm going to do."

CHAPTER SIX
THE RESISTANCE

The Derian Resistance met in a cellar in a particularly dilapidated part of Felrin. As they approached on the wagon, Cole was shocked at the sight of a row of three terraced houses whose roofs had caved in on themselves like piles of discarded junk.

"This is terrible," Cole murmured as he noticed a child crouched in the doorway of a building with all its windows cracked, hanging loosely like fangs. "People shouldn't have to live like this."

"They have no other choice," said Meeka. "We're lucky that weaving has been passed down in our family for generations. Mum can create rugs even finer than those in Alfar and our wagon is still in good shape."

"It wouldn't take much," added Piog, his brow beaded with sweat from the parched heat of the day. "If the pony went lame, or Mum got too sick to work, or if the palace stopped supplying food for our town, that would be it. One thing goes wrong and we end up living out here, making do with scraps."

"That's why we have to do this, Cole," Meeka finished.

Cole swallowed and nodded. He was nearly as old as Piog and Meeka but he had never needed to get a job or had to worry that he and his family might lose their house or go hungry.

Piog parked the wagon in a narrow alley and tied the pony to a post so rotten that it looked like a good tug could snap it. Meeka led the way through the makeshift shelters to a building that looked like it had once been a large inn. Now, it was nothing more than two tumble-down walls, a sign that said 'The Emerald Oak' and a lot of banked-up boulders. Cole would have thought the place deserted completely, were it not for the thin stream of smoke trailing from the chimney.

"The Oak was looted years ago," Meeka muttered, "so it makes the perfect hiding place. We're going down there." She pointed to the corner where the two remaining walls met. A thin, hessian sheet was strung out to create a sort of roof, and beneath it there was an old trapdoor, the wood smoothed from the tramping of many feet over many decades.

Meeka and Piog pulled the rusted handle and a blast of light and noise bubbled up like the cooking pot in Yognar's cottage. It even smelled like the stale stew.

As Cole followed the twins down the rickety ladder, he wondered if what he was doing was sensible. Mum and Dad wouldn't think so, and Liam and Mara would be too strong and smart to get into this kind of trouble, but Cole was Cole, and he was learning that this was a very Cole-ish thing to do. The Derians needed help and Cole could help in a way that no other Derian could. The people of this world might be forbidden from entering the palace, but the king himself had invited Cole to return any time he liked.

The basement of the Emerald Oak wasn't exactly comfortable, but it was a vast improvement on the derelict streets above. Warm lamps glowed around the walls and a smoky fire burned in a small grate. There were about twenty Derians sitting on benches or leaning against the uneven walls, talking earnestly. They wore faded cloth in muted colours, but their faces wore something even more telling – every pair of eyes was marked with crow's feet and every mouth turned downwards at the corners, symptoms of living under the harsh rule of a power-mad tyrant. As three armour-clad Derians, each with stringy, shoulder-length hair, slunk along the shadowy wall, Cole heard the words 'curse that Enk' and 'ours by rights' and 'now or never'.

Redbush the squirrel stood by the fire, poking the meagre flames with a metal stick. When he saw Piog, Meeka and Cole heading over, he nodded a greeting. He didn't seem surprised to see Cole there.

"Glad you made it," Redbush continued, his nose twitching. His voice was low and gravelly, which Cole did not think was quite how he imagined the squirrels in the local park sounding.

"I thought you said that there were loads of people coming," Piog complained.

"Many have," said Redbush sadly, the tip of his tail flicking restlessly from side to side. He pointed out a few small groups of tired-looking Derians. "Those two are from Narwan" – Cole saw a pair of ruddy-faced young women with thin scarves over their noses and mouths – "and these have come all the way from Blacksand." He gestured towards three men who sat around a small table with their heads together. "But they come here at great risk to their safety. If they were stopped and questioned, or if the mountain conditions became too treacherous..." Redbush sighed and his whiskers twitched. "Others have chosen not to take the risk. Can we blame them?" Then, he stepped away from the fire and called the meeting to attention.

"Friends," he began. The gathered Derians fell quiet and turned to listen. "What you have been told is true. An elseworlder has returned the seal of Felrin to our world."

Cole shuffled uncomfortably. It was strange to hear himself talked about like this. He didn't know if anyone realised who he was, besides Piog and Meeka.

"Many of you will know the stories, passed down through generations, of King Enk's lifelong ambition to collect every single magical seal in Deriuss." At this, many dark and disgusted glances shot around the room, and one man from Blacksand actually spat on the ground at the mention of the king's name.

Redbush continued. "I have spent many years finding out all that I can about Enk and, for those who have not heard the stories, this is all I know.

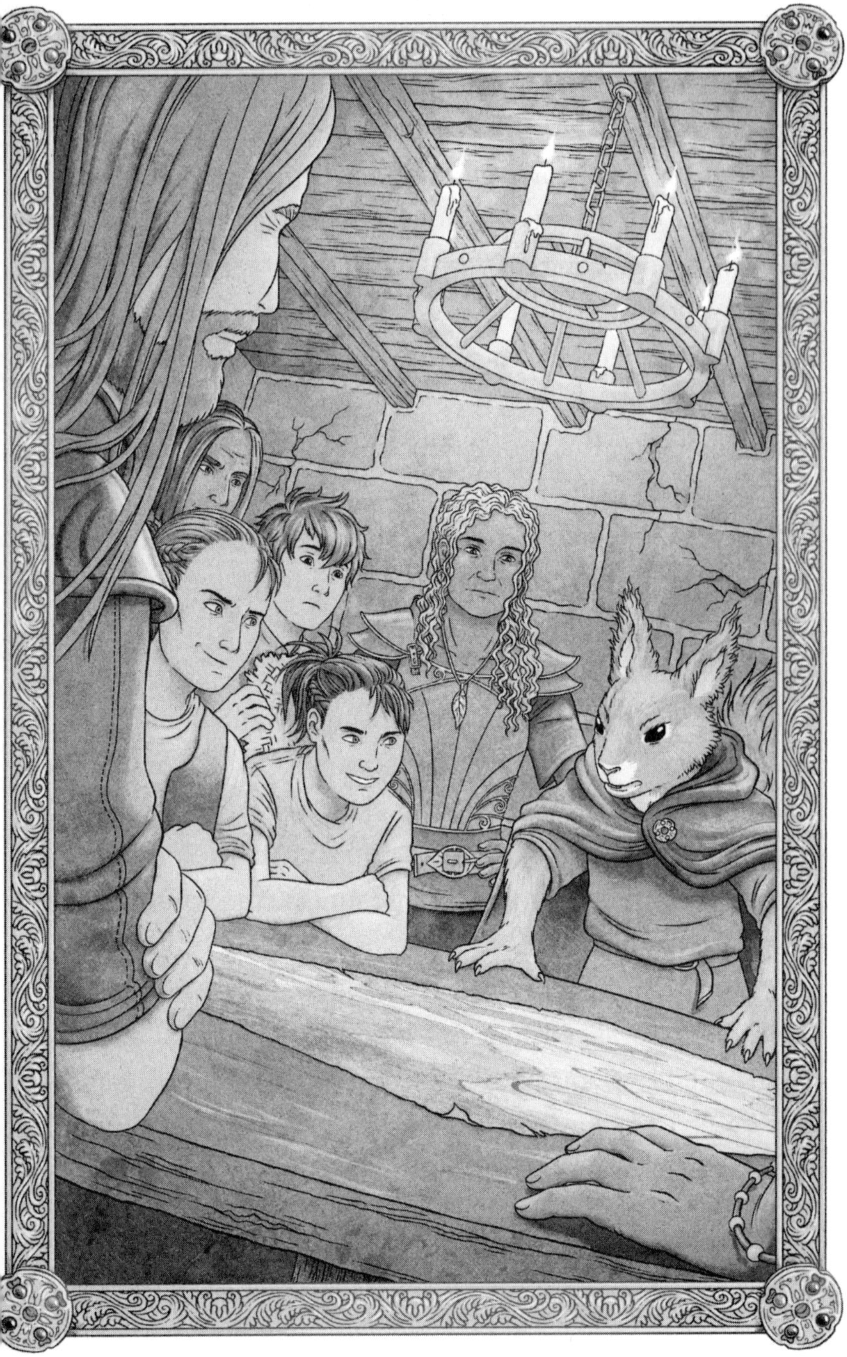

"In the first years of the king's reign, many settlements caught wind of Enk's intentions and elected to hide their seals away. Each town and village sent a messenger to an elsewhere world and the seals were hidden in places where they were unlikely to be touched before the king's reign ended. Knowing that Deriuss would have enough magic to last until the end of his natural life, the Derians waited."

The silence in the room was absolute. The Derians were all watching Redbush with rapt attention, their wide eyes reflecting the flickering firelight twenty or more times over. Some nodded in recognition; others, like Piog and Meeka, were visibly on the edges of their seats.

"However," he continued with a thinly-veiled note of scorn in his voice, "those in the elsewheres who came across the seals were unable to keep their curiosity at bay. The moment an elseworlder failed to resist the lure of a shiny object and touched any seal, the king's creatures were able to find it.

"The Derians of old had not counted upon this, and their plan failed. Sometimes, decades would pass between the return of one seal and the next but, gradually, Enk's collection grew. The more seals he crams into that monstrous contraption of his, the stronger the life force inside Alfar becomes, and the longer he is able to rule us all."

Cole's face had grown incredibly hot. He had been impressed by Redbush's commanding presence and his ability to speak so well but now, he felt hollow. This time, he had been the foolish elseworlder unable to resist touching the seal – but how was he to know what would happen? He hadn't even known that Deriuss existed before yesterday. He shifted his weight so that he was hidden behind the twins, as Redbush continued into the attentive quiet.

"King Enk now has every single Derian seal in his palace. This – will – not – do." He drew out every syllable, each one dripping with fervour. "Who can say what this could mean for Deriuss? Never before in history has earth magic been compressed and contained in this way. It must be stopped."

"Hear, hear!" cried the assembled throng.

"Which is why we must plan to enter the palace tomorrow night, during the king's celebratory ball. It will be dangerous – very dangerous – and there are many risks."

"We'll get torn to pieces by his wolves!" a small woman called, looking fearful.

"How will we get past the gate?" asked a large man in an apron.

"Ah," said Redbush calmly. "That is where we will need the help of Piog and Meeka's new elseworlder friend."

Cole's heart seemed to freeze in his chest. Redbush knew who he was and why he was here.

A great deal of murmuring broke out in the small basement room, and Piog and Meeka moved aside to reveal him. He blanched under the stares of every pair of eyes. "Uh, hi," he said, his voice unnaturally high-pitched.

Redbush spoke to him from the front of the room, fixing him with a steely gaze. "I can only assume, since you have chosen to stay in Felrin today, that you wish to be of assistance to us."

Cole's habit of talking when he was nervous was what saved him. "Yes," he garbled. "The king told me that I could come back whenever I wanted to learn magic and – and I thought that might help." The words had flown out of him so quickly, he thought that it was a miracle that anyone had understood them.

Redbush looked appraisingly at Cole. "Indeed. I do believe that you could be useful, and I have a plan." He addressed the room at large. "During the ball, the king and all his court will be distracted. Drinking, gorging, dancing – I have seen it. If I know anything about Enk, he likes to show off his accomplishments. The seal will be on display, you mark my words. Its addition to the well will be the main event and that is what we need to stop."

At that, voices clamoured.

"But *how* will we get into the ballroom during a party?"

"Won't it be under heavy guard?"

"How can we trust the elseworlder after what he's done?"

Redbush held out his hands to calm the questions. "It won't be easy, but that's why we're here. To formulate a plan." Then, he turned to the twins. "Piog, Meeka – do you trust this boy?"

The twins gaped at each other and then at Cole, before nodding determinedly as one. "Cole's our friend," said Meeka. Cole felt a rush of gratitude toward them.

"Very well," said the squirrel. "Cole, you will be crucial to our success. Piog, bring out more chairs – it's going to be a long night."

*

After much talk, Redbush had taken Cole's arm in his paw and led him and the twins to a quiet spot, away from the crowd.

"If you are staying in our world for another night, I'll walk you and the twins back," he said kindly.

"You can sleep in the wagon!" Piog added.

Darkness had fallen when Cole and Redbush tramped towards the cottage. The meeting had gone on long into the night and, by the end, Cole's head was reeling with thoughts of secret entrances and covert signals, of disguises, traps and ambush. He tried to focus on the part that he would play. Piog and Meeka lagged behind, arguing insistently about who would be the one to actually swipe the seal. Neither seemed to recall that their part in the plan did not involve either of them stealing anything.

Redbush had been silent since they left the meeting and Cole had tried hard not to babble at him. He had spent hours detailing everything he could about the palace and listening to the clamour of voices in the Resistance meeting, and it had taught him a lesson in patience.

At last, Redbush spoke. "I'm an elseworlder like you," he said quietly, his head tucked down.

Cole gaped at him.

"A human," he continued. "I was on the beach with my brother when I stumbled into this world by accident, as so many have before me and since. My brother and I were arguing. We were always arguing. We both wanted to play with the same ball but we couldn't bear to play together. My brother threw the ball away and, when I chased after it, I found myself on the mountains just outside of the king's domain – Alfar. When I reached the palace, it was just like you described it, though there were fewer animal servants in those days.

"I met the king. He showed me his wonders, impressed me with his magic and promised that I, too, could learn magic, if only I were to eat the teoquat fruit."

The squirrel paused. Cole waited without speaking; Redbush seemed so lost in memories that he didn't want to disturb. The thick, sweet smell of the teoquat fruit seemed to fill the air around them, and all Cole could think of was how lucky he had been to escape the king's palace.

"And then?" he prompted finally.

"I thought, *that'll show my brother. I'll have magic and he'll have nothing.* I didn't think about what the cost would be. I didn't even think about the king's warning that I could never leave this land. I would have magic and, with magic, I could do anything. So I ate the fruit."

Redbush held out his furry paws and flicked his bushy tail. "Then, I became... this."

"You mean all those mice and foxes and badgers up at the palace..." Cole said breathlessly, "They're all..."

"Every one of them," said Redbush gravely. "All elseworlders like you and me, tricked by the king. Some have been brought along in the scuffle for a magical seal, just like you. Others posed no threat to the kingdom and merely fell through portals by mistake."

"And did the fruit give you magical powers?"

Redbush gave a grim smile. "No, it did not."

"Why not?"

"Deriuss is crying out for its magic to be used, Cole. The teoquat fruit is saturated with the magic that the earth cannot distribute: a product of trapped, mutated natural energy. For Derians like the king, eating the fruit brings about an unnatural and unbridled power. To elseworlders, however, it brings only dismay."

"Why can't you go home?" Cole mused aloud.

Redbush sighed. "In theory, there is no reason that we elseworlders who have been changed could not return to our world – but why would we, when our own families would not recognise us?" There was a silence, during which each became lost in his own thoughts. Then, the squirrel continued. "Besides which, I was very young when I entered this world. I have spent many years in this land – am known by a new name, as so many of Enk's oldest servants are – and I doubt that I could remember now where the portal to my world lay back then. Only the king's scouts know the best places to find portals to elsewhere worlds. I believe that you met one such creature on your arrival."

Cole scowled. "Yeah, I did – a mouse," he grumbled. "Greedy, thieving –"

"Don't judge him too harshly," said Redbush. "Enk holds a great deal of power over his subjects, and mice are very capable of squeezing into small places such as those where portals may be concealed."

"But you got away from him," said Cole. "You escaped

to Felrin?"

"Eventually, yes. Squirrels are tricky like that. If I had become a sloth, I would still be up there serving drinks. The teoquat fruit reveals the inner nature of a person and makes it visible."

"That explains the wolves," mumbled Cole. "They seem more than happy to do Enk's bidding."

"True," said the squirrel, "but they are also weak-willed creatures. Enk has a harder time controlling some creatures but with others, he can use his magic to force them to do his bidding."

Cole gasped. "I've felt it!" he said. "I felt my hands and my feet doing things I didn't tell them to."

Redbush nodded. "I believe that, until now, he has only had the power to push us gently towards actions that we had already considered in our minds – but I shudder to think how powerful he could become when he places the final seal in that well."

There was a very long pause, during which all the awful possibilities hung in the air between them.

"We'll get it back," said Cole. "I promise."

His voice was steady but inside, his stomach churned and an unpleasant thought danced jeeringly in his head. He knew by now that the king was a power-hungry, manipulative liar. He knew that the king kept the Derians in poverty and hoarded magic for himself. Yet, still, a little part of him had held onto the thought that he, Cole, was special – that the king had, in fact, seen something in him and had wanted Cole as his magical apprentice. Now that he knew it was just a trick, he knew something else too: he wasn't special. He was just an ordinary boy. Did he have any chance at all of helping the Derians?

He squashed the thought to the bottom of his brain. It was too late now. He had to try.

CHAPTER SEVEN
AN UNEXPECTED TURN

Cole stood outside the gates of Alfar, in the middle of the clearing. Bright light from the vaulted windows of the palace cut through the night in shades of pink and purple and green. He was quite alone, wearing the same thin jumper and dirty trainers he had on when he first crawled through the portal. This was part of the Derians' plan: to pretend that he had had a change of heart and decided to return to the palace for the promise of magic. There could be no evidence that he had ever met a Derian outside Alfar, let alone joined their plot to retrieve the seals from the king.

His part of the plan was simple enough to remember. The Resistance had gone ahead and taken their positions all around the palace. Cole was to distract the king and the guards for just long enough that the Resistance could sneak into the palace through various, carefully organised means and gain access to the teoquat orchard. Piog and Meeka would deliver crates of Resistance members disguised as Yognar's latest weaving produce and, with Cole keeping the guards busy, the group would overpower those wolves who remained. It was risky, but Cole had given a good explanation of the layout of the ground floor of the palace. For his part, all he had to do was keep the king talking for a long time without being forced to eat the teoquat fruit.

Cole rubbed his palms together. They were damp from the ever-present heat saturating the air. The gates seemed deserted, and he was just wondering if he should simply push them open and go inside when two wolves shifted out of the shadows on the top of one of the nearby towers.

Cole cleared his throat. It was very dry. "Uh... hello," he called. "Can – can I come in, please?" It sounded very childish and he regretted it instantly.

To his surprise, however, one of the wolves vanished from the top of the tower and, slowly, the great gates to the city began to open. Surely, it couldn't be that easy...

A fairly small wolf with brown-grey fur met Cole as he stepped through the gateway. "State your business," he said matter-of-factly.

"The – the king is expecting me... I hope."

The wolf didn't even blink. He spun on the spot, dropped to all fours and led Cole towards the great marble steps.

Cole couldn't believe his luck and, as he stepped through the lush palace gardens and began to hear faint music, he became light-headed with momentary relief. "Is there a party going on? I didn't realise. Will he be busy? It's just that I was here a few days ago and the king said that if I ever wanted to return and see the city... I mean, you don't visit another world, a world with magic, every day, do you?" he rattled on as they ascended the stairs and followed the hallway along to the great throne room.

Once inside the palace, Cole was overwhelmed by the noise and colour of the ball. Dizzying music spiralled through the air and the guests stomped and spun and pranced together in twos and sixes and twenties as if part of some huge pattern that was too big for Cole to see. The air was thick with smells: sweet, sharp and spicy all at once. Cole wanted to see and taste everything and leap into the pattern of the dance but each time he tried to find the essence of the music, it slipped away from him.

Some guests wore animal masks or feathered headpieces or flowers that cascaded over their shoulders. It might have been difficult, therefore, for Cole to tell who was a guest and who was an elseworlder tricked to stay in servitude by King Enk, had it not been for the fact that there were no animals dancing. They were all weaving between the guests, serving drinks or else lining the walls of the throne room with platters of food. The string quartet was made up of two lizards, a rabbit and some kind of giant anteater.

He dragged his thoughts from the mesmerising dance and tripped over his feet as they pushed through the crowd. He had come here for a reason. He had to keep his head straight, to carry out his part in the Derians' plan and win their freedom from the king. If he could take the stage and convince the king that he wanted to eat the teoquat fruit, surely that would stall the celebrations for long enough to get the Resistance inside and give them their chance to act – but it would be a race against time.

Something flashed, dazzlingly bright, at the far side of the room. As the wolf led Cole closer, he began to make out what it was. On the large, panelled dais was a pedestal and on top of the pedestal was the seal of Felrin, polished to a high shine so that the jewels sparkled. Cole's heartbeat quickened. The seal was not yet part of the well. Redbush had been right – Enk was waiting for his chance to show off. Beside the pedestal, he could see the king sitting on his throne, watching the dancers with casual interest.

As they moved towards the dais, Cole saw how tight and fierce the security was. Standing sentry around the great hall were no fewer than ten wolves wearing snarls on their faces, and no one danced too close to the dais. *Not to worry*, thought Cole. *Soon, I'll be up there and all their eyes will be on me, not the Resistance.* He began to prepare his first words to King Enk in his head.

The wolf from the gate marched along the edge of the room and towards the side of the dais – but then, it turned a sharp corner and Cole found himself being taken down a gloomy-looking corridor.

"Where are we going?" asked Cole, a little panicky. "I'm sure the king wouldn't mind if we just..."

The sight of what was waiting for him stopped him in his tracks. Standing in the middle of the corridor with a wide sneer on her face was Serla, the grey-streaked wolf captain in the red cloak. She looked completely unsurprised to see him.

"Good evening," she said silkily. "To what do we owe this pleasure?"

After allowing himself a moment's shock, Cole rallied and said, "Oh – hello. I was just telling your – your colleague, here, that I have an invitation from the king."

Serla raised an eyebrow and, when she did not respond, Cole continued. "Well, he – he said that I could come back any time."

The wolf's face relaxed into a smile. "As it happens, His Highness did mention that you might be dropping by."

"Oh," Cole said. "Brilliant!"

"Indeed," replied Serla, and she beckoned him towards her. "The king requested," she continued, "that should such an event occur, I was to ask you to wait for him just in here." Smiling broader still, she placed a paw on Cole's shoulder and spun him round to face a heavy door which led off the corridor. The brown wolf opened it and bowed low, with a barely concealed grin, as the pair stepped inside.

Before Cole was a set of spiral, stone stairs. The chamber was as dark as the night outside, with only a few flickering sconces to light the way down into the gloom. An eerie cold swept up the staircase towards Cole and, as his eyes adjusted and the wolf's grip tightened on his shoulder, he saw that the walls lining the steps were hung with chains, manacles and gruesome-looking instruments made of rusted metal.

A bead of cold sweat skated down Cole's back and he shivered. His shoulder was now being dug into so hard by Serla's long claws that he looked down at it, half expecting to see blood.

"Did you really think," came a whispered growl in his ear, "that an old rug and a stupid straw hat could hide you from me? Or that I'd let you just wander back into the king's halls after spending two nights with that squirrel and his friends? Fool!"

Cole's heart stopped. Shock reverberated through his head like a crashing cymbal.

"Get in," Serla snapped, giving Cole a shove. He tried to dig his feet in and brace himself against the floor tiles, but they were polished smooth.

"I can't go in there!" Cole protested as he slid nearer to the dark staircase. "I haven't done anything wrong." With a firm push from the wolf, he clattered down the winding steps with the wolf close behind him. "My family are waiting for me. They'll come after me. They won't let you get away with this."

Hot breath tickled his neck and pointed teeth snapped by his face. Cole yelped and hurried down the last few steps into the room below, clutching his ears to keep them from being bitten off. As his foot reached the grimy floor of a dark dungeon chamber, Serla's claws curled over his shoulder and steered him across the room.

"Have a nice stay," laughed the wolf, throwing him into a dank cell and clanging the door shut.

"Wait!" Cole grabbed the iron bars and shook them. "Come back! Let me explain!" But the howl of laughter was already fading to nothing as his captors vanished upstairs. There came a loud *thunk* from the slamming door, then silence.

The green torches illuminating the dungeon gave off a poisoned light that seemed to drip off everything it touched. It was a circular room lined with many small cells with gated fronts. Cole shivered. The warmth from the world above clearly couldn't penetrate the thick walls, and the air was polluted with the stench of damp stone and animal droppings. Cole squinted through the dark, looking for any other prisoners behind the bars of the adjacent and opposite cells.

"Hello?"

He heard scuttling and wheezing and scratching, but whoever the other occupants were, they were keeping to the shadows.

Cole sank onto the driest patch of straw he could find and put his head in his hands to think about what Serla had said. *She knew.* She had seen him in the town square – and that meant that King Enk would know, too, that Cole had not gone home but instead had been talking to Redbush and the Derians. There was no way that he would believe that Cole had come back to learn magic, now.

No sooner had the thought crossed his mind than the door at the top of the stone steps creaked open again, and the sound of finely made shoes click-clacked down into the dingy chamber.

King Enk was dressed in robes of royal blue which trailed behind him as he walked. His long, gangling frame was made even taller by the presence of a solid-looking golden crown, which sat so comfortably above his white hair that it looked as though it might have grown there. In his long, pale fingers was the seal of Felrin, its jewels dancing in the low light.

The king took a few careful steps across the dungeon floor to look into Cole's cell. Cole stood up automatically, but then wished that he hadn't.

"Cole," said the king in a supercilious voice. "Cole, Cole, Cole." He clicked his tongue like a disappointed mother hen and Cole found himself reddening with irritation. "We got on so well the last time you were here. What happened?" The king bent to sit down and Cole realised with a start that a red velvet chair had appeared under him, so that he sat peering at Cole like a visitor on a hospital ward.

"I'll tell you what happened," said Cole, breathing fast. "I spoke to some of your people, Enk. I saw how they're living and what you've taken away from them."

King Enk chuckled. "But you have been listening to lies, dear boy. Surely you would not take the word of vagrants and criminals –"

"They're good people!" Cole cried. "They're kind and honest and they're suffering! *You're* supposed to be their protector."

The king's smile vanished in one blink of his dark eyes. "My people do not know what is best for them," he snarled. "The magic in this land belongs to me. It is my job and my right as king to decide how the power in this land should be distributed."

"You're not a king!" laughed Cole, a little surprised by his own boldness. "You're a bully! You're afraid that your people will rise up against you so you keep them powerless and penniless, and you hide in here behind your big stone walls. If anyone is foolish enough to stumble into your world, you trap them here because you're so terrified of sharing your secrets. You've taken the magic of this world and twisted it into something unnatural and ugly." Cole could tell that he was rambling, but he knew that he had to keep the king talking for as long as possible.

"You have no idea what it is to be a king," Enk sneered. His dark eyes had become black in the greenish light and he suddenly looked a lot less regal. "You are a boy – a meddlesome, irritating boy who doesn't know when to keep his mouth shut." He sighed and shook his head. "I showed you my magic, I offered you the chance to be something great, to share all this power –"

"Power?! I've seen what 'power' you give to elseworlders. What did you hope I would turn into?" Cole felt bitter resentment rising up in him at the memory of how Enk had made him think for a second that he was something special. "You might be able to conjure food and chairs and who knows what else out of thin air, but nothing about it is real. In all my time in Deriuss, the most real, honest food I've had was dirty, gritty and made with love."

The king smiled into the silence and looked calmly into Cole's eyes. Cole glared back.

After a few moments, the stalemate ended and Enk got to his feet. He fingered the golden seal delicately and said, "It matters not. By the time this ball is over, I will have completed my collection. I will be the master of all the power that this world has to offer and you," he added, smiling mildly down at Cole, "will stay here. You will eat the teoquat whether you like it or not, and you will be grateful for the life that I will give you inside my *big stone walls*."

With that, the king swept up the polished steps and out of sight and the door thudded heavily behind him. His chair had vanished.

Cole's heart was pounding in his chest and his insides felt hollow from the rush of adrenaline and rage. He slid down the wall of his cell and felt hot, angry tears spill down his face. Wiping them furiously on his sleeve, he thought bleakly of the members of the Derian Resistance – of Piog, Meeka and Redbush. Had they made it into the palace? Had he bought them any time at all with his ranting at the king? Enk would be returning to the ballroom at any moment and, if they were even there, the Resistance would be standing by, risking everything, waiting for Cole to cause a distraction that would never come. He was furious with himself for allowing himself to be tricked and now, he was stuck down in the dungeon with no way to help them or even to warn them.

"That was brave of you."

Cole jumped. He blinked and rubbed his eyes again, wondering if he was hearing things.

"What you said – it was very much needed."

A voice was coming from one of the cells on the other side of the dungeon, and Cole scurried to the bars which made up the front of his cell. "Who's there?" he called.

On the other side of the poorly lit room, something was moving in one of the barred alcoves. Slowly, a creature moved into the glow of the nearest lantern.

A long, smooth snout appeared first, followed by two intelligent, tired-looking eyes and a mane of fine, tufted hair. Cole watched as the figure of a large primate emerged and a pair of hands with long, delicate fingers wrapped themselves around the cold bars of the cell door.

Cole was reminded very much of being at the zoo. After a

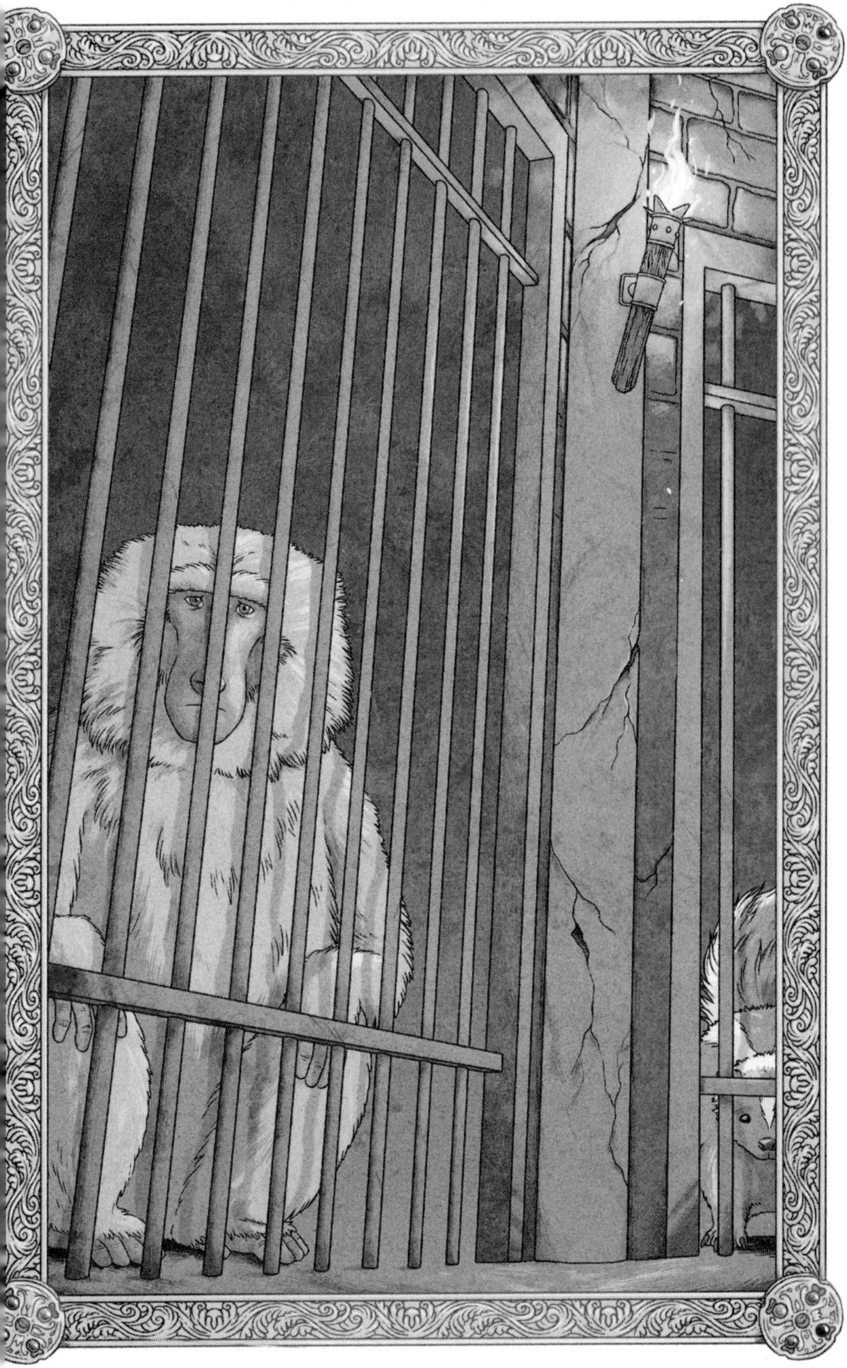

few seconds, he realised that he was staring with his mouth hanging open slightly, and shut it quickly. Wondering hastily what the best thing was to say to an oversized monkey on your first meeting, he settled for, "Why are you in here?"

The baboon sighed. "For the same reason as you, elseworlder. I chose to defy Enk." He had a solemn, slow voice and gazed at Cole sadly. "My name is Jonas."

"Cole," said Cole.

Jonas nodded. "I saw you on your first visit to the palace. This" – he glanced at the cell to his left – "is Molly."

Momentarily confused, Cole turned to look at the next cell over and his mouth dropped open again, for a second creature had appeared there.

Cole recognised it instantly as a skunk. Eyes like two black beads peered out of a small face and vivid white stripes ran from the tip of its nose to its back, where they fanned out into a huge, bushy tail.

"Hello, Molly," Cole said kindly, for she looked quite frightened. Her paws were fiddling with her fur and she was unable to look Cole in the eye.

Jonas came to her rescue. "Molly was six years old when she stumbled across the seal of Narwan."

"*Six?!*"

The baboon nodded. Cole noticed that these animals seemed to have kept their human names, unlike Redbush. He imagined trying to resist the promise of limitless magic when he was only six years old and a new surge of anger rose up in his throat. Molly had never stood a chance.

"Enk has been able to play mind tricks on the creatures in his service for many years," Jonas explained. "Those of us who have been here the longest have grown accustomed to it but we are also able to resist him more as time goes on. We are all in here because King Enk has no idea what to do with us while he is unable to control us completely."

Cole remembered what Redbush had said to him the previous night.

"*I shudder to think how powerful he could become when he places the final seal in that well.*"

"I doubt you'll be in here for long," he said gloomily. "Wait," he added, for realisation had just dawned on him. "You said 'all'. 'We are *all* in here', you said."

"Indeed," replied Jonas.

Cole stared around at the cells to his left and right and took a step back in surprise.

Creatures of all shapes and sizes had appeared at the bars of their tiny cells, peering out at Cole as though he were something wonderful. Cole saw a beaver, a kangaroo, a lynx, a boar, a spaniel and a screech owl, each pair of eyes flickering in the dim light.

"We have all been punished for disobeying Enk's orders," Jonas explained.

"Wow," Cole breathed. "Well, this is fantastic!"

The animals lining the room looked at one another in bemusement.

"It is!" said Cole. "You're all outside of Enk's control – you can fight!"

Molly the skunk gave a fearful squeak and hid behind her tail; Jonas continued to gaze at Cole. "We have been fighting all our lives," he said. "Enk is surrounded by wolves and he has too much magic."

"After tonight, he'll have even more," said Cole. He had to make them understand. "After tonight, you'll have no hope of resisting his magic and nothing will stop him from ruling over you forever!" When they did not respond, he continued, beseeching them all in turn. "Don't you want to be free? Don't you see that it's now or never?"

"But what about the wolves?" asked the boar.

"He'll use his magic against us," worried the lynx.

"Of course we want to be free," Jonas said firmly.

Cole sighed. His breath misted in the air in front of him and he thrust his hands into his pockets to keep them warm. "It's OK to be frightened," he said. "It's normal. The king is powerful and has many skills that we don't have, but you won't be on your own. I came here today with people from all over Deriuss, people who have come to fight. My friends Piog, Meeka and Redbush are waiting for me, and if I don't get out of this dungeon –"

He stopped because the animals had suddenly started to shift around in their cells, casting excited glances at one another. "What?" he asked.

"Redbush is here?" asked the owl. "You mean, the squirrel?"

Cole blinked. "Well, yeah," he said, completely nonplussed.

The murmuring broke out again and Jonas said, "Redbush is well known among the palace animals. He is the only elseworlder to have eaten the teoquat and escaped from Alfar. The wolves search for him often but he has never been found. It was he who inspired many of us to rebel in the first place."

Nodding encouragingly, Cole clutched at this new development as though it were a lifeline. "Well, he's here and he needs our help. Redbush has given you hope but he is no more impressive than you are. All he has is bravery. If you have the courage to stand up beside him and fight, we can defeat Enk *together*."

Silence followed. The animals looked as though they were chewing over Cole's words carefully.

"If Redbush has returned," the kangaroo said at last, "and he believes in this elseworlder, then we must help him to fight." One by one, the occupants of a few nearby cells nodded in agreement and the dark cellar suddenly seemed a little brighter.

"That is all very well," said Jonas calmly, "but how are we going to help? In case you hadn't noticed, we are a little hampered by these iron bars."

Cole scowled at the door of his cell. Hands still stuffed into his pockets, he took a few paces around, scanning the dingy chamber for anything which might help them.

"I could try to kick the door down," suggested the kangaroo.

"That would make too much noise," said the lynx.

"I could scratch at the bars," offered the spaniel.

"What if I run at the lock?" added the boar.

"I could try to gnaw at the hinges," said the beaver.

"No, no," said Jonas. "These bars cannot be broken with strength. If they could, we would have broken out by now!"

"There has to be a way," Cole said, his head swimming with possibilities. "There just *has* to b-"

He stopped. In his frustration, his fists had thumped the bottom of his jacket pockets and a soft *clink* had come from them as his knuckles had struck cold metal. Carefully, he pulled out a small object and held it up to the light.

III

Grandma Jenny's attic keys glinted dully in Cole's hand and he turned them over. He fingered each one gently: the one that had let him into the old, cracked door at the top of the stairs, and the other key, which had seemed to have no use.

"You'll be needing these."

Surely not...

Cole hardly dared to hope, but it seemed foolish not to try. As he walked to the door of his cell and reached through the bars around to the front, a giddy giggle rose up in the back of his throat. It waited there until he had inserted the silver key into the lock and turned it, and only when the door to Cole's cell swung open with a creak did it burst from him, turning into a hoot of disbelieving laughter.

CHAPTER EIGHT
THE KING'S BALL

In the great ballroom, the party was in full swing. Guests in masks and elaborate costumes mingled among the animals carrying trays and serving drinks; waves of aroma from expensive perfumes and delicious canapés filled the air. A lively song in a major key rose up from the string quartet in the corner of the hall, just about audible over the excited chatter of the attendees and the clinking of glasses, and caused the whole crowd to sway and pulse as one in time to the music.

Around the edges of the space, the slick forms of Serla and her wolves waited patiently for any sign of trouble. Up on the dais at the far end of the room sat King Enk, gazing serenely down over his celebration with an expression of satisfied ease.

The partygoers all blended into one colourful mass. Had anyone cared to look more closely, however, they would have noticed that, hidden here and there in the throng, around a dozen men and women were standing alone, stiller and more quietly than the rest. It would have been clear, too, that their clothes were slightly dirtier and more poorly fitting than those of the people around them and that, every now and then, they shot one another furtive glances across the hall, each one more stricken-looking than the last. Watching more carefully still, one might have noticed that a particularly poorly dressed dancer had pointed, red ears poking out from under his headdress.

The Resistance were here. Redbush the squirrel stood among the well-to-do residents of Alfar, his eyes upon the king as the party moved around him. Every few seconds, he glanced towards the nearest door or wolf, as though waiting for something or someone, but nothing occurred that seemed to satisfy him. After around fifteen minutes, he frowned and began to stare intently at the marble floor.

More seconds turned into minutes. Enk stirred in his chair and the men and women secreted around the room fidgeted uncomfortably as it occurred to each of them that what they were waiting for had not arrived. They all looked, panicked, at each other and then at Redbush, who avoided their gaze pointedly. His nose twitched and he scratched his chin, deep in thought.

Without warning, King Enk was on his feet. He crossed the dais to stand beside the seal of Felrin, which glittered on its pedestal.

"My friends," he called, and the room fell silent almost at once. Every head turned as though pulled by a string and the musicians halted their song abruptly. "Citizens of this most noble kingdom, it brings me great happiness to see you all here this evening." He beamed down at them all.

Redbush stood amid a large cluster of people in the centre of the ballroom. The men and women watching the squirrel for their instructions saw him duck his head low and begin to move. Blankly, their eyes followed him as he made his way slowly through the crowd towards the front, stopping every so often to scan the room.

"This is a wondrous occasion," Enk continued. "For many, many years, we have awaited the return of the seal of Felrin." The king stroked the seal on its pedestal with one long finger. "With this final addition to our wonderful Alfarian well, we have secured the prosperity and stability of this great nation for centuries to come."

The crowd in the great hall clapped enthusiastically. Now that they had all stopped dancing, however, it became easier to see the one cloaked figure that was making its way gradually towards the dais. His eyes on the king, Redbush weaved between gilded headdresses and ducked under arms adorned with bangles and holding goblets.

"It brings me great comfort," said the king, "to know that the magic of Deriuss is now safely stored in this palace, away from hands who would put it to poor use."

Redbush crept further forwards and came level with the grey-streaked wolf, Serla, who stood straight-backed and pale against the wall to one side. Her head turned in his direction and he froze.

"Never in living memory have all of these seals been united in harmony," Enk was saying.

Redbush and the white wolf stared at one another for a moment, and the wolf's yellow eyes narrowed. Redbush took one more tentative step towards the dais.

"Tonight, you and I are about to witness something truly remarkable."

Everything happened in an instant. The enormous wolf

plunged forwards into the crowd, scattering guests far and wide. Redbush leapt out of the way so quickly that his roughly made headdress fell off and his huge, bushy tail bounced out from under his cloak. The Alfarians made exclamations of surprise and indignation, and the wolves around the edges of the room sprang to attention. Each one made a move towards Redbush but found their path blocked by a member of the Resistance. The dozen Derian men and women jumped, incensed, at the wolves, blocking the squirrel from view. Piog and Meeka were clinging on with all their might to one wolf's fur, and it swatted at them in irritation.

It was pandemonium. Redbush bounced on all fours between scuffling wolves and Resistance members, toppling trays of drinks and terrified, shrieking guests. Serla tore through the crowd, dividing it down the centre as her pack growled and barked at their assailants. Everywhere, cloaks ripped, glass shattered and yet more wolf guards appeared from the teoquat orchard courtyard to enter the fray.

Standing above all the brawling, King Enk watched with an expression of abject fury. As Redbush bounded up onto the dais and reached out a paw in a desperate attempt to take the seal of Felrin from its pedestal, the king clicked his fingers with a sharp *snap*.

Vines as thick as pythons burst through the wooden floor and snaked themselves around Redbush's chest and tail, binding him to the steps where he stood. The loud crashing of broken floorboards caused the tussling men, women and creatures around the hall to fall still and turn towards the cause of the noise. A single glass fell to the floor and smashed, then there was silence.

Inches from the glimmering pedestal, Redbush struggled furiously against the vines but they held him tight. Breathing heavily, King Enk stepped forwards to address the room at large again. "This illustrates my point perfectly," he said, his voice rising with anger. "Deriuss is about to enter a new era of power and plenty, and we must safeguard our future against those who would seek to destroy it."

Redbush twisted against his binds and attempted to shout up at the king, but all that came out was a muffled yell as yet more vines forced themselves around his mouth. Members of the Resistance who had darted forwards to assist him were caught by waiting wolves, and they wriggled and shouted in earnest.

"Down with Enk!"

"Resist!"

The king's dark eyes flashed with panic and anger as he looked around at his animal servants and the men and women of the Resistance. "Let this serve as a lesson to anyone who fancies themselves as a hero." He clicked his fingers and pulled from thin air a magnificent silver sword encrusted with rubies and sapphires. "The might and magic of Alfar is great, and you are no match for it." As he spoke, Enk raised the heavy sword above his head and the muffled screams of the Resistance members filled the hall.

From his hiding place behind the dais, Cole watched wide-eyed as the king's sword reached its peak above his golden crown and prepared to fall. Icy sweat ran down his neck and he felt as though his insides were trying to push themselves out through his mouth.

"I will have order and you are neither strong enough," Enk shouted over the noise, "nor quick-witted enough to stop me."

The Resistance were still struggling against their wolf captors and Redbush stood as stiff as a board, unable to move an inch. As though in slow motion, the king's silver sword swung through the air. Down it came in a whirl of silver, red and blue – and then it stopped abruptly.

Panting and pale-faced, Cole stood defiantly between

Redbush and the king, his hands on the hilt of the king's sword and pushing upwards with all the strength he could muster. The crowd gasped. A flash of light reflected in the sword's shining blade flitted across the king's face, and he no longer looked serene or kingly – he looked mad.

"You," he hissed, his voice dripping with hatred.

"Me," said Cole. His breathing was short and sharp, having dashed across the dais in the nick of time, and his knees felt as though they might give way at any moment, but he stared up at Enk and forced himself to speak. "You won't do any more damage to this kingdom," he said, "because your people have had enough."

The king laughed maniacally and leered down at Cole, putting an immense weight behind the huge sword without seeming to make any effort at all. "And what power," he asked sardonically, "do the *people* have to fight against me?"

Cole heaved harder still and felt one of his knees collapse underneath him. "None," he croaked, pushing as much air through his lungs as possible, "but you're wrong. They didn't need super strength, extra-special intelligence or magic to stop you. They just needed enough courage to *do the right thing.*"

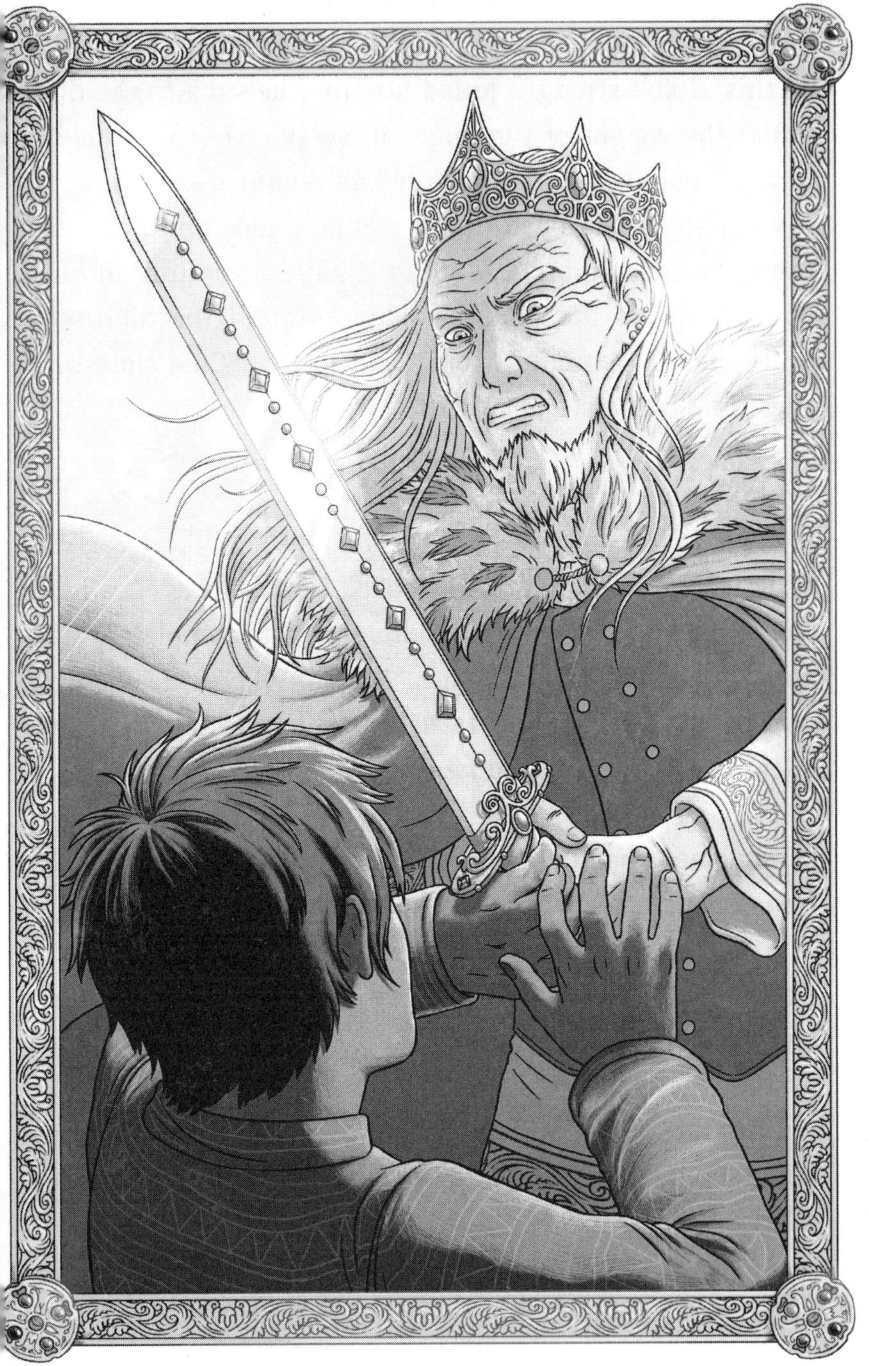

At this, Cole's strength failed him and he sank to the floor under the weight of the magical weapon. The silver blade lurched wildly, and then King Enk regained control of it. A wide smile stretched across his pale face and he raised the sword once more, swinging it without hesitation back down towards the dais, cleaving through the air above Cole's head. Trembling from head to foot, Cole closed his eyes tight and held his breath –

Nothing happened.

After a second or two, Cole looked up with his eyes half-closed and saw that the king was standing completely still, staring blankly at his empty hands, where the magical sword had been moments before. Blinking stupidly, Enk clicked his fingers but, again, nothing happened.

A movement behind Cole told him that Redbush was also free. The vines and the sword had vanished.

Cole allowed himself to breathe. Anticipation and anger were forcing King Enk's chest to heave up and down and his eyes, as wide as dinner plates, searched Cole wildly for some explanation. Cole merely smiled and stood up as a new, pattering sound broke through the silence behind him.

Through the parted crowd came the scurrying of many hooves and paws, accompanied by gasps from the watching Derians. Eight figures appeared from the now unguarded teoquat orchard; Cole watched as the king's gaze rose to the newcomers and his bearded jaw dropped.

Standing in the centre of the magnificent hall was a group of creatures of all shapes and sizes, their tails, talons and tusks quivering. Jonas the monkey stood tall at the front, a satisfied look settling on his tired features. In every pair of paws were two or three golden, bejewelled seals. Hidden by the fighting in the great hall, the imprisoned animals had emptied the magic well of its seals and the king's unnatural spells were broken.

The whole room held its breath and looked from the animals to the king, who stood frozen beside his throne. Suddenly looking sallow-faced, he made to lunge savagely at the pedestal and the seal of Felrin, but found that Redbush the squirrel was spinning it leisurely between his paws.

Enk stared, incandescent with rage, at Serla and her wolves. "*Well*?!" he screamed. "What are you waiting for? Get –"

The command was left hanging in the perfumed air, as Enk seemed to choke on something that the room could not see.

Before their eyes, the king's face was turning milky white and his skin was becoming tight over his features. Lines drew themselves across his face and his hair thinned until he was almost bald, and then he was shrinking, shaking and twisting as he became smaller and more ancient. Every year of his impossibly long life suddenly seemed visible and, within seconds, he had shrivelled into a frail old man, no more than two feet tall, half-buried in his robes at the foot of his throne and still shrinking. The king's golden crown hit the floor with a *thunk*. Finally, all that was left of King Enk, ruler of the land of Deriuss and master of its magic, was a small mound of ash.

For a few moments, no one could think of anything to say or do. Cole glanced around the ballroom, where wolves and Resistance members were still poised mid-fight.

Redbush moved beside him and turned to face the room. When he spoke, his voice sounded clear and confident. "We do not want to fight," he said, gazing around at the wolves and the residents of Alfar. "We wish only to return the magic of Deriuss to its rightful place: the lands which belong to our people. With your help, we can turn Deriuss into a fair society where everyone can live and work alongside one another."

When no one objected, Redbush began to give instructions. Members of the Resistance tentatively collected the seals that had been pulled from the well. Serla the wolf stood aghast, staring at the space where her king had stood, and her pack stood poised around the hall, waiting.

Cole watched as Redbush approached her. It struck Cole how very brave the squirrel was to walk right up to the creature that had hunted him for so many years, and he held his breath. Serla was clearly thinking the same thing, as she growled and dropped her front end low to the ground, baring her gleaming teeth. Redbush came within inches of her fur and spoke in a calm undertone. Although Cole could not hear his words, he saw the wolf slowly stand, round up her guards and skulk after Redbush through a side door.

The room gradually filled with noise and movement as the people of Alfar began to pick one another up from the floor. Resistance members and the dungeon animals celebrated with wine and food swiped from tables that had not been upturned, while some servants bustled through and began to clean up, seemingly out of habit. Piog and Meeka came hurtling up onto the dais, beaming at Cole brightly, before pouncing on him for a rib-crushing hug.

CHAPTER NINE
A NEW BEGINNING

The following day, Cole was standing in the teoquat orchard when Redbush joined him.

"Good morning, Cole."

"Hi," Cole replied.

"I trust that you slept well."

Cole nodded. "I've never slept in a palace before."

It had been very late the previous night when Cole and the Derians had finally fallen into beds in the palace, and it was now mid-morning. Sunlight was, once again, streaming in from above the small courtyard so that the white columns and arches glowed. The rest of the scene had changed dramatically, however. The teoquat trees which had pulsed with energy and life during Cole's last visit had blackened and wilted, their branches dry and cracking away from the walls. Leaves and vines which had once been fresh and green now lay crisp and brown on the ground. Where the space had thrummed with life just days ago, the courtyard was now as still and silent as the grave.

Redbush sighed as he looked around. "We have a lot of work to do," he said sagely. The squirrel walked slowly once around the magical well, which no longer bubbled with life-giving power. The basins were empty and, all around the base of the strange fountain, large holes showed where the various Derian seals had once sat.

The animals whom Cole had met in the dungeon had performed their parts perfectly. Once the Resistance members had been recognised and the ball had descended into chaos, the orchard guards had been drawn into the ballroom. Immediately, the animals had wrenched out as many seals as they could hold in their paws and, within seconds, the garden of teoquat trees that had been feeding upon the concentrated magic had been transformed. The fruits adorning the branches had now shrivelled to a fraction of their original size and had become as hard as stones.

"I thought that you might become human again," Cole said, thinking aloud, "when the seals were removed." He watched Redbush inspecting the dry well, and wondered how he was feeling now that he had won his freedom.

"Yes, I think that a lot of the animals had hoped that would be the case," said Redbush finally. "Alas, not. We are not from this place. The earth magic that was contained in those fruits is what gives life to everything in Deriuss, and it seems that it has made us a part of the natural world."

"What will you do now?" asked Cole.

Redbush smiled. "Well, with Enk gone, the people of Deriuss are free to replace the seals in their local wells and begin to live off the land again. For my part, I intend to remain in Alfar."

"Here?" Cole asked. He was surprised; he much preferred the quiet, humble town of Felrin to the lavish city of Alfar, and had expected Redbush to feel the same way.

"Absolutely. The people here will need to adapt to life without a king and Alfar will be surviving on only a fraction of the earth magic that it is used to. They will need some guidance, I think."

"And what about the elseworlders?" Cole wondered. "They're still animals. What will they do?"

Redbush gave a sad smile. "Some might stay," he said. "They know no other life, and they are welcome to remain in the palace if they wish, but others may choose to travel the kingdom. The most important thing is that they are now free to make that choice."

The pair stood in the crumbling orchard for a long time, each lost in his own thoughts, until a noise behind Cole made him turn around.

Piog and Meeka were walking across the courtyard, their pockets full to bursting with pastries and cakes and looking immensely pleased with themselves.

"You all right, Cole?" Piog said, handing him a cup of something warm and sweet. "Here. It's plum grog, and it is so, so good."

"Better than hot grains, at any rate!" Meeka said thickly through a mouthful of bread.

Cole took the cup with a nod, and stopped to breathe in its fragrance before allowing just the softest sip to pass his lips. It was good. It was better than good. It was friendship, and love, and the value of the earth. "Thanks, it's delicious." He hesitated, feeling a twinge of sadness, and then said, "I suppose that I'd better try to get back home."

"Not just yet!" cried Meeka in a tone of astonishment. "You'll stay for the party, won't you?"

"Party?" asked Cole, bewildered.

"'Course! You can't deny Mum the chance to feed you properly!" Piog laughed.

*

The news that Enk's rule was over had spread like wildfire across the kingdom. Before long, everyone had heard the story of the king's demise and celebrations seemed to be the order of the day – but not before the people of Deriuss had chosen their new leader. No one, including Cole, could think of anyone better placed to lead the kingdom into its new age than Redbush, and after much persuasion, he had agreed. The squirrel had, however, insisted that representatives be chosen from every town in Deriuss, so that each could have a vote on any important decisions that were made.

Back in the town of Felrin, a feast was being prepared using all the excess food that the palace could provide.

The animal servants were so grateful to Cole and Redbush that they had bent over backwards to supply them with anything that they could ask for.

"Come on! Come on! Out of the way."

Yognar had been so busy directing events all morning that she hadn't even noticed the groups of children who were swiping treats off the tables laid out in the streets. Every time she turned to top up the bread, fruit or cheese, there would be significantly less than a minute before. Her face was turning a severe shade of beetroot and Cole thought that it was best to get out of her way before he ended up wearing the pail of milk she carried.

"Let's get to the well, Mum," said Meeka. "We don't want to miss it!" Judging by the cream smeared across her face and the wedge of cheese poking out from her tunic, she had been the worst offender. "Here," she whispered to Cole, handing him a bread roll, which he pocketed.

As they walked through the streets of Felrin, which had become significantly noisier and busier overnight, Cole spoke. "So, the seal's back?"

"Redbush is bringing it down from the palace," said Piog. "Some of the other elseworlders are delivering the rest back to the other towns and cities."

They turned a corner into the town square, which was as hot, dusty and dry as ever. It was filled with people, just as it had been the last time Cole had seen it – but the atmosphere could not have been more different. The town bell was clanging and people stood chatting animatedly, gathered around with the stone well in their midst and an air of excited expectation. News of Cole's part in the king's downfall had trickled through the town, and people stopped to point at him or wave cheerfully as they went past.

"Redbush is here!" a young girl squealed, and the crowd was hushed at once.

Sure enough, Redbush was approaching the stone well at a leisurely pace, and in his paws was the seal of Felrin. He was flanked by a group of five or six elseworlders from the palace, and in their midst was someone whom Cole had not expected to see on this day of celebration: the grey-streaked white wolf, Serla.

Redbush hopped up onto the well so that he could be seen by everyone. "We have returned from the palace," he said, his voice clear and loud. He took a long pause and scanned the faces in the expectant crowd. Murmurs broke out at the sight of the wolf and Redbush raised a paw as if to silence them, but then brought it down gently onto the wolf's shoulder. "This is Serla, and you all know who she was."

The murmurs became angry cries, but Redbush did not falter. "She was an elseworlder like me, and I ask you to forgive her."

"Never!" someone hidden in the crowd shouted in an almost instant reply.

Redbush allowed the people to grumble and shout and flatly refuse, until the din eventually died away to silence. When he replied, he did so with a kindness that even Cole could see had been lacking during King Enk's reign. "This is a special place," he said. "I was lost for many years, but thanks to all of you, I have found something to believe in and something to be. If I can be chosen to lead, she must be allowed to change. If we deny her this chance, we are no better than Enk."

The crowd were stunned to silence by Redbush's words. Cole felt uneasy as he thought back to his own treatment by the wolf and the countless orders that Serla and her pack must have carried out in the service of Enk. Looking at the wolf now, however, he saw that there was a sadness in her eyes and felt inclined to give her the chance to be something better. While the people around him shifted and murmured uncomfortably, Cole stepped through the crowd and approached the wolf. He took Serla's paw in his own hand, reached into his pocket and pulled out the bread roll given to him by Meeka.

"Here," he said. Serla frowned and gripped the roll lightly, then Cole twisted it until it tore in half. "What better way to make friends than over a meal?"

Redbush nodded appreciatively as the expressions in the crowd softened slightly. "And now," he said with an air of grandeur, "without further ado..." He reached down and slipped the seal of Felrin into the waiting well with a satisfying *clunk*.

The effect was immediate. The well's foundations seemed to shudder like an engine starting up, and a faint gurgling could be heard somewhere below them. Then, without warning, a jet of perfectly clear water shot out of the top of the well and began to gush down the sides so that Redbush was forced to jump out of its way. A few seconds later, a ripple which seemed to start in the centre of the well rumbled under their feet and continued outwards through the square. As it disappeared beyond the houses and streets, the sky above their heads turned from stark blue to a cool, milky grey and a light rain began to touch upon the noses and foreheads of the townsfolk.

The citizens of Felrin were beside themselves with delight. Piog and Meeka ran up and down the square, holding out their hands to catch raindrops, while Yognar gazed up at the sky with tears cascading down her cheeks. Friends and family were embracing; children were splashing in the water that was tumbling out of the well and onto the floor.

"Cole," said Redbush turning to him, "thank you. You will never know how much your bravery has helped the people of Deriuss."

"I didn't do anything, really," said Cole.

Redbush smiled. "Do you really think so? The way I see it, you survived an encounter with the king where others had been trapped. You spent time listening to the people of Deriuss; you joined the Resistance instead of returning home; you escaped from the king's dungeon with eight prisoners; you saved my life and you brought balance to this land. I wonder if all of this would have happened if somebody else had come through that portal."

Cole didn't know what to say. He wasn't sure whether it was due to the smiling faces all around them or the kind words that Redbush had spoken, but he felt as though a small fire had started somewhere inside him, its flames feeble but sending warmth right through his body

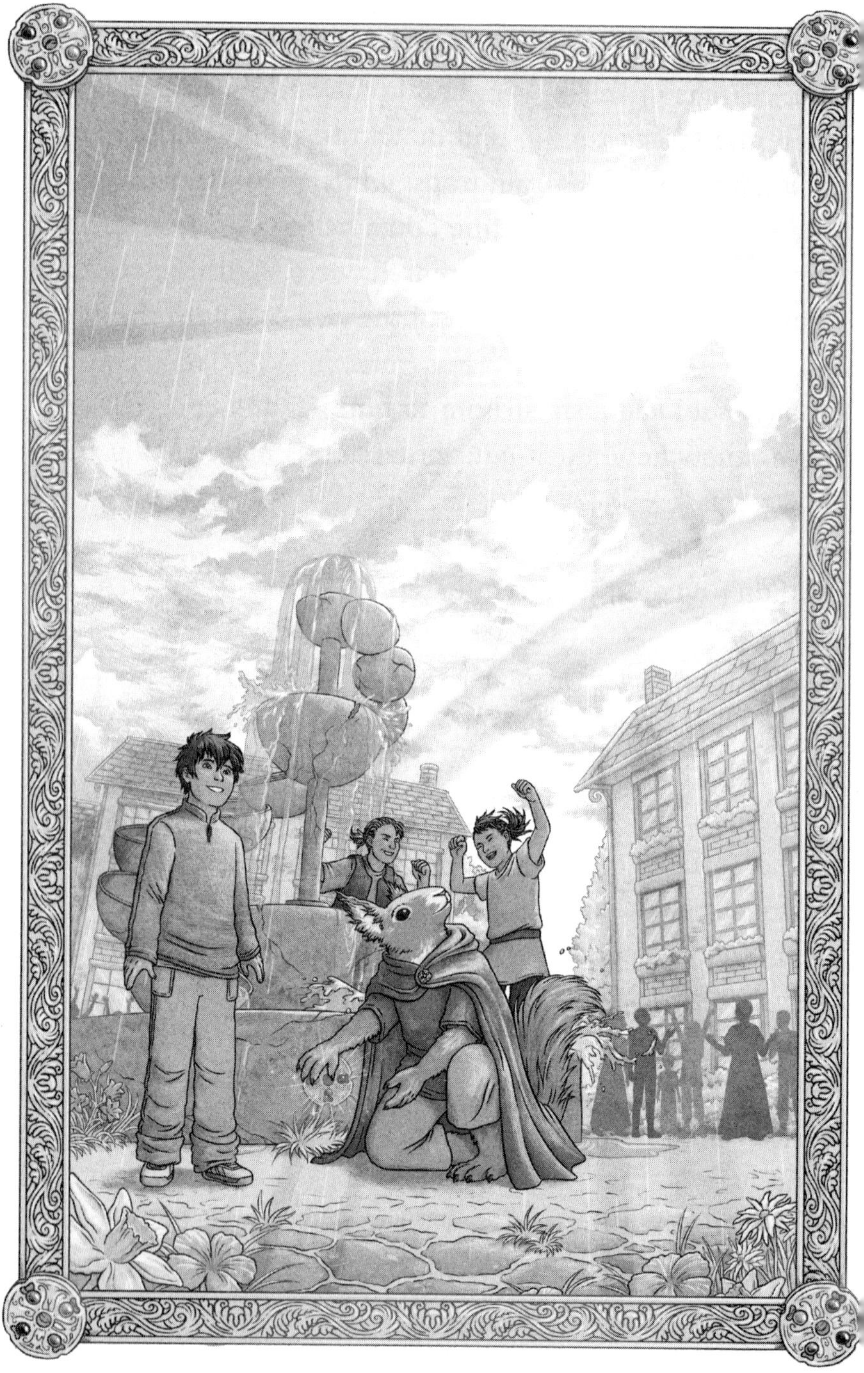

to his fingertips.

Silence fell between them for a moment. Finding his voice, Cole said, "I'm sorry that you'll never be able to go home."

Redbush turned away from Cole and looked around at the people celebrating with their families and friends, before staring up towards the palace on the mountainside. "I rather think," he said contentedly, "that I am already home."

CHAPTER TEN
THE SHORT CRAWL HOME

The celebrations and feasting went on long into the evening but, once the novelty of seeing Piog and Meeka stuffing an impressive number of grapes into their mouths wore off, Cole didn't quite feel like partying any more. The residents of Deriuss were delighting in the earth magic that was flowing back into the world; halfway through the afternoon, a thin, life-giving mist had swirled and danced up into the sky and, with it, a vivid spectrum of light had coloured the horizon. As the magic had settled once more, the dusty fields had instantly sprouted tiny green shoots, and the trees had begun to sway and whisper with new leaves. In the space of a day, the memories of King Enk's rule had been washed away and a new dawn had begun.

Under the cover of all the merriment, Cole slipped away from the party and down the street to Yognar's cottage. He stopped for a moment and watched as a vine adorned with flowers sprouted from the ground and snaked its way up the outside wall. Deriuss was truly the most wonderful place that he had ever seen and it was once more becoming the world that its people deserved. Here, he had found friends and a purpose, so why did he feel so hollow? Piog and Meeka were kind and Yognar was attentive and caring. In Deriuss, he had everything he needed to be his true self.

"You're welcome to stay here, you know." The voice took him by surprise for only a second, but the warm tone told him that it was Yognar. She, too, had left the party and stood leaning against the side of the cottage. "The people of Deriuss will be forever in your debt and, if you like, there is a place for you with us."

Cole smiled at her, but shook his head. As much as he now felt a part of this world, it would never be a replacement for life back home. He missed the sound of Mum's voice, the smell of Dad's baking, listening to Mara's facts and hearing Liam's music. Taking a closer look at the flowers growing outside Yognar's house, he breathed in a familiar scent: lavender.

"I'm sorry, Yognar, but I have to go home. My grandma set

me a job to do and I can't let her down."

Yognar simply smiled and said, "I'll fetch the twins. They'll get you home."

*

The wagon ride back to the portal was quiet. Piog and Meeka had eaten almost their entire body weight in cheese and cake and their eyes kept dropping heavily. Cole wasn't quite sure what to say to them.

"Hey, I – uh..."

"We'll miss you."

Cole couldn't see which of the twins had said it, but they both had their eyes on him. He nodded soundlessly, because his mouth seemed to be refusing to form words.

Piog, who was driving the wagon, pulled the pony to a stop. He looked at Cole and smiled but it seemed like a struggle. "We're here."

Meeka tapped her fingers lightly on her knees and huffed. Her breath danced, warm and white in the chilly night air, and she looked out into the treeline, which had now been transformed. A thick, lush forest awaited them, and Cole could almost feel it breathing.

He heaved himself out of the wagon. Although he was certain that leaving Deriuss was the right decision, it didn't make it any easier. He went to speak, but the twins grabbed him and pulled him into a tight, group hug.

"Thank you," squeaked Piog.

"Yeah," agreed Meeka, "and sorry about the whole kidnapping thing."

"Don't worry about it," smiled Cole. He turned away and headed towards a familiar-looking tree, ready to begin the short crawl back.

There was a problem.

In the place where the portal had once been were nothing but tangled tree roots and dirt. When he had first followed the mouse through, the hole had seemed impossibly small, but it had widened as he had crawled. Now, all that waited for him was compacted earth.

"I can't find it!" Cole cried.

The twins dropped to their knees and all three searched among the undergrowth, but there was nothing to be found – no dusty attic, no boxes of treasures, no lavender perfume. Was this Deriuss's way of trying to keep him?

Suddenly, it hit Cole that the choice to leave Deriuss may never have been there at all. Would he be stuck here forever like Redbush? What would his family think when he never came down from the attic? It had already been several days and nights and they would be out of their minds with worry. It was all Cole could do not to cry.

"Hello."

A shrill voice spoke from behind the trio, trembling slightly with an emotion that Cole couldn't quite place. He looked up and saw that, standing on a tree stump to the right of the wagon, clutching its tail, was King Enk's personal thief: the mouse.

"You!" Cole gasped.

The little mouse bowed its head, but didn't run. Even when Piog jumped up and ran over to the stump, it remained still. "I'm sorry," it said.

"*Sorry*? You're the whole reason I ended up here." Cole

lost himself for a moment and felt full of anger towards the creature who had stolen the seal of Felrin. Then, he remembered how he had forgiven Serla, and how he had made new friends in the two people standing beside him. As much trouble as coming to Deriuss had caused him, Cole could not ignore the fact that the lives of all the people of this world had been improved by him doing so. The seal had been returned, magic flowed through the lands once more, and there was a leader in the palace who would keep the peace for years to come.

"What shall we do with it?" Meeka was saying. She rolled up her sleeves and cracked her knuckles menacingly.

"Leave it," Cole told her, standing up and walking over to the creature. "What's your name?"

"Lightfoot," said the mouse, with a rueful glance up at Cole.

"Well, Lightfoot," Cole said. He breathed heavily, took one last look at the exposed roots of the tree and then made for the wagon. "Come with us. There's food in town and I'm sure we can find a spot for you to sleep."

Lightfoot looked up at Cole but, rather than gratitude, his face wore surprise. "You're not going home?"

"I can't," said Cole. "The portal is gone." He swallowed hard against the lump that had formed in the back of his throat.

Suddenly, Lightfoot's face exploded with delight. "Not for me, it isn't!" Without hesitation, he sprang off the stump and dived into the dark of the tree roots. Cole and the twins heard excited chirps and, before they even had time to blink, the writhing tentacles of the tree had unfurled to reveal a shadowy space. Carried on a warm breeze, the smell of flowers and chocolate biscuits reached Cole's nose.

Lightfoot returned, standing up to his full height beside Cole's knee and beaming.

"How did you do that?" Cole asked.

"Mice have a way of getting into spots where others cannot."

"You're not kidding," Cole laughed. There was no stopping him now. The portal home was open and every part of his body was now telling him that this was the right thing to do. "Well," he said, looking at his three companions. "Bye, then."

"Come back soon," smiled a waving Piog.

Cole hesitated, but chose not to correct him. In the back of his mind, he knew that it was unlikely that he would ever be able to return to Grandma Jenny's house once she had moved away. So, he chose his words carefully.

"Take care."

As he crouched and pulled himself through the damp tunnel, the smells and sounds of Deriuss disappeared like raindrops on a river.

*

Cole stood in Grandma Jenny's attic with the rain lashing down on the skylights. Dust swirled in the air and, from downstairs, the warm smell of freshly baked biscuits called to him. Images of another time, another place and another life blurred through his mind, as though he were in the first few moments of waking from a dream. He had lived every memory as if it were from the most exciting book, but that was all they were now – just another one of Cole's tall tales.

As he walked to the doorway leading to the landing, Cole wondered why, after three days, the attic had not been cleared yet. If he had been lost for so long, why would his family be making biscuits?

"Hello?" he called, but was met by only silence.

Cole took the rickety stairs down past the music room, where an acoustic guitar lay flat on the carpet, and past the study, where no fewer than eight books lay open and scattered across the floor.

There was no sign yet of his family. Perhaps, the moment someone had realised that he was missing, they had given up on tidying to try and find him. A hollowness smacked Cole in the stomach as he realised fully how worried his family must have been. Taking the final flight of stairs three at a time, Cole dashed into the living room, and was met by the sight of Grandma Jenny in her chair, with Mum, Dad, Liam and Mara gathered around her.

"Cole!" Mum said.

"It's OK, it's OK. I'm back," Cole announced, putting his arms around his mother. "I'm so sorry. You must have all been so worried!"

"We were actually just deciding who was going to eat your biscuit," said Mara.

Cole looked at her blankly. "I – what?"

"Dad made some. I don't think it was going well in the shed..."

"I wanted this half," Liam moaned. "It has more chocolate chips – but Mara said that her first one was smaller than mine."

While his siblings resumed what Cole assumed had been a long-running argument, Grandma Jenny reached onto the plate. "Now, now, no one but Cole will have this. I think that he deserves it. Off you go and finish up."

One by one, Cole's family scattered until it was only he and Grandma Jenny left.

What was happening? Cole had been gone for ages but everyone was still tidying up the house – in fact, it seemed as though only a few minutes had passed since he had first stepped into Deriuss three days before – if he had done so at all. He sat perfectly still and rubbed his chin in confusion, with the feeling of being lost for words that had become a lot more familiar recently.

"Here you go, love," Grandma Jenny said, handing over the biscuit. Cole picked it up and savoured it slowly. The food on his adventures had been wonderful, but there was nothing quite like Dad's homemade chocolate chip biscuits.

When he looked up, he saw that Grandma Jenny was eyeing him closely. She looked from Cole's dirty trainers to his slightly sun-browned nose and unwashed hair. Then, she smiled.

"Everything OK, love?" she asked. "Have you finished with my keys?"

Through his biscuit crumbs, Cole opened his mouth to tell Grandma all about Lightfoot, the seal and everything that had happened in Deriuss, but stopped himself. He knew that Grandma would have listened to it all, but this felt like a story that was just for him. "Yes," he said. "They came in really handy, Grandma. Thanks." He looked into her grey eyes and tried to communicate what he was feeling as he handed Grandma's keys back to her.

They sat together, he on the arm of her chair and she wrapped in her blanket, watching the rain tap against the windows. The tangled branches of the oak tree in the garden swished rhythmically from side to side. It had already been a very long day for Cole, and he was just about to close his eyes when, between the leaves of the tree, he saw a small creature leap from one branch to another. It was a red squirrel.

Cole flinched and went to speak, but Grandma Jenny interrupted him. "You look cold. Here." She pulled the blanket off her legs and wrapped it around his shoulders. Instantly, he was warmed, but there was also something suddenly recognisable about the design woven into the blanket. As Cole gazed down at the fabric now draped over his arms, he felt a familiar urge to step right into the scene depicted there.

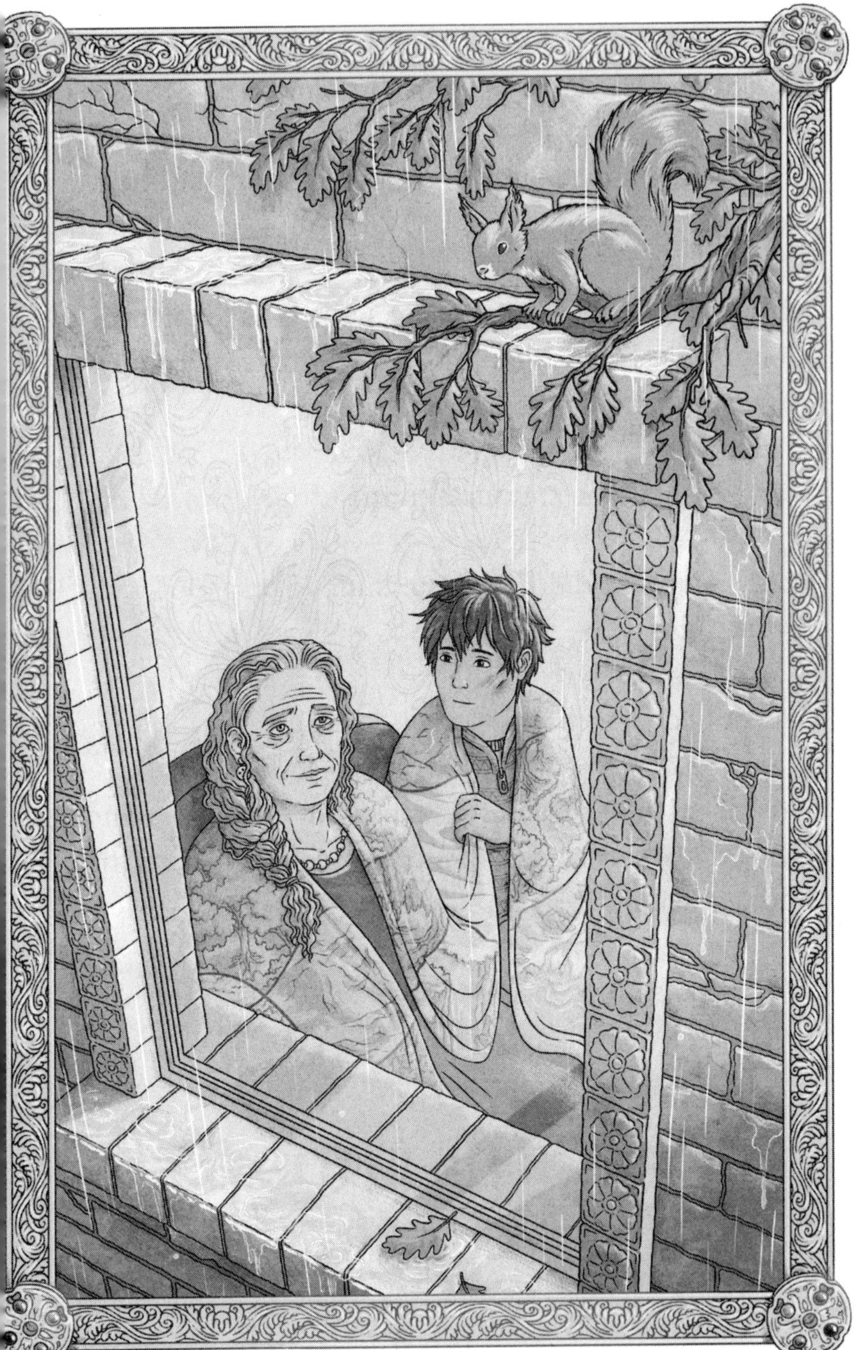

"Grandma, where did you get this blanket?"

"A dear friend made it for me, my love, but that was long, long ago."

He looked at her then, and she smiled. As Cole opened his mouth to ask the thousands of questions burning in his mind, Grandma Jenny beat him to it.

"Did you find any treasures in the attic?"

Cole nodded. "I did find something very special – but I'm afraid I lost it."

"Put it back where it belonged, I hope."

Flashes of his adventures appeared in Cole's mind: his friends, his battles and the forever-changed world that he had left behind.

"Yeah," he smiled. "Yeah, that's exactly what I did."

THE END

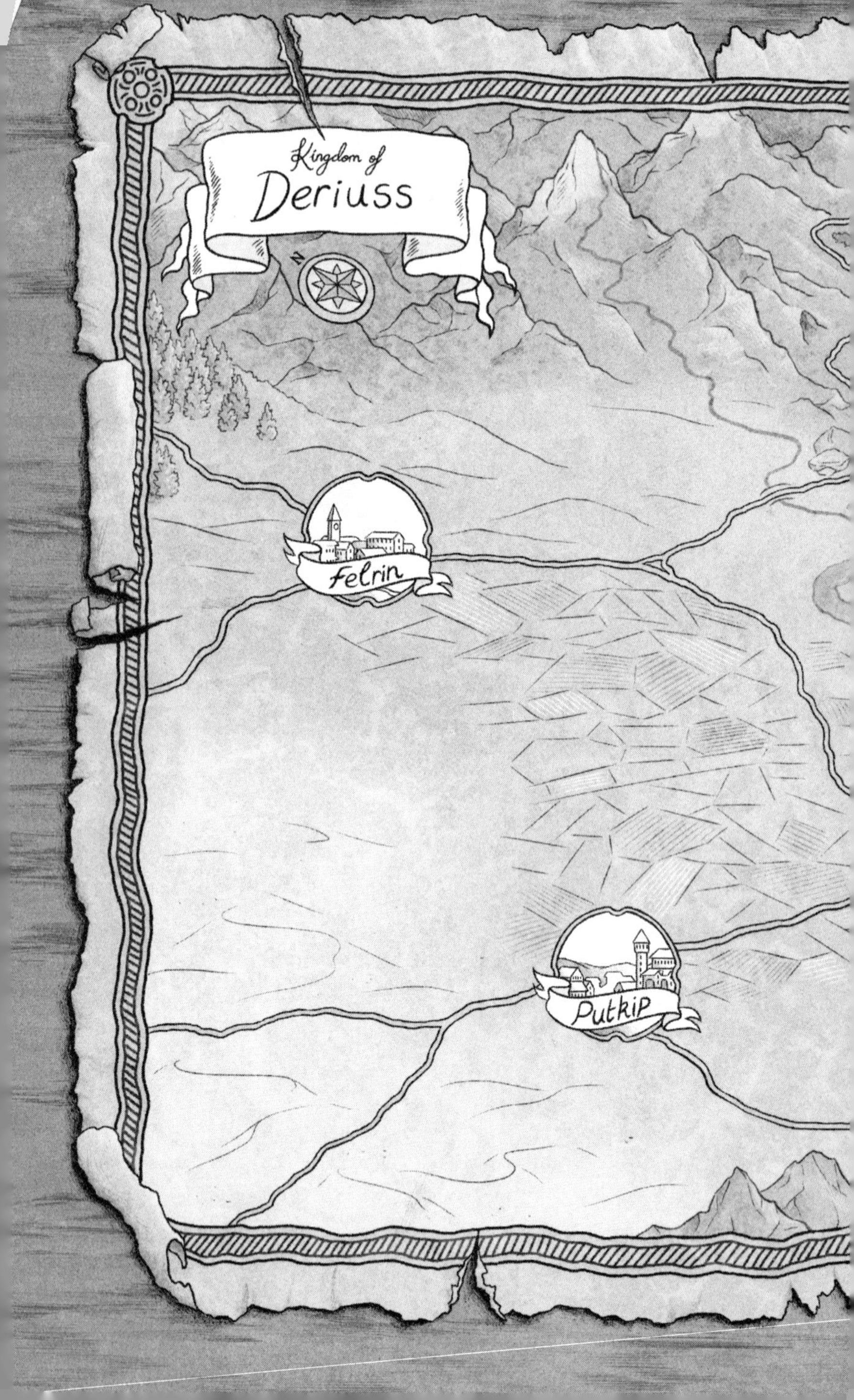
Kingdom of
Deriuss
N
Felrin
Putkip

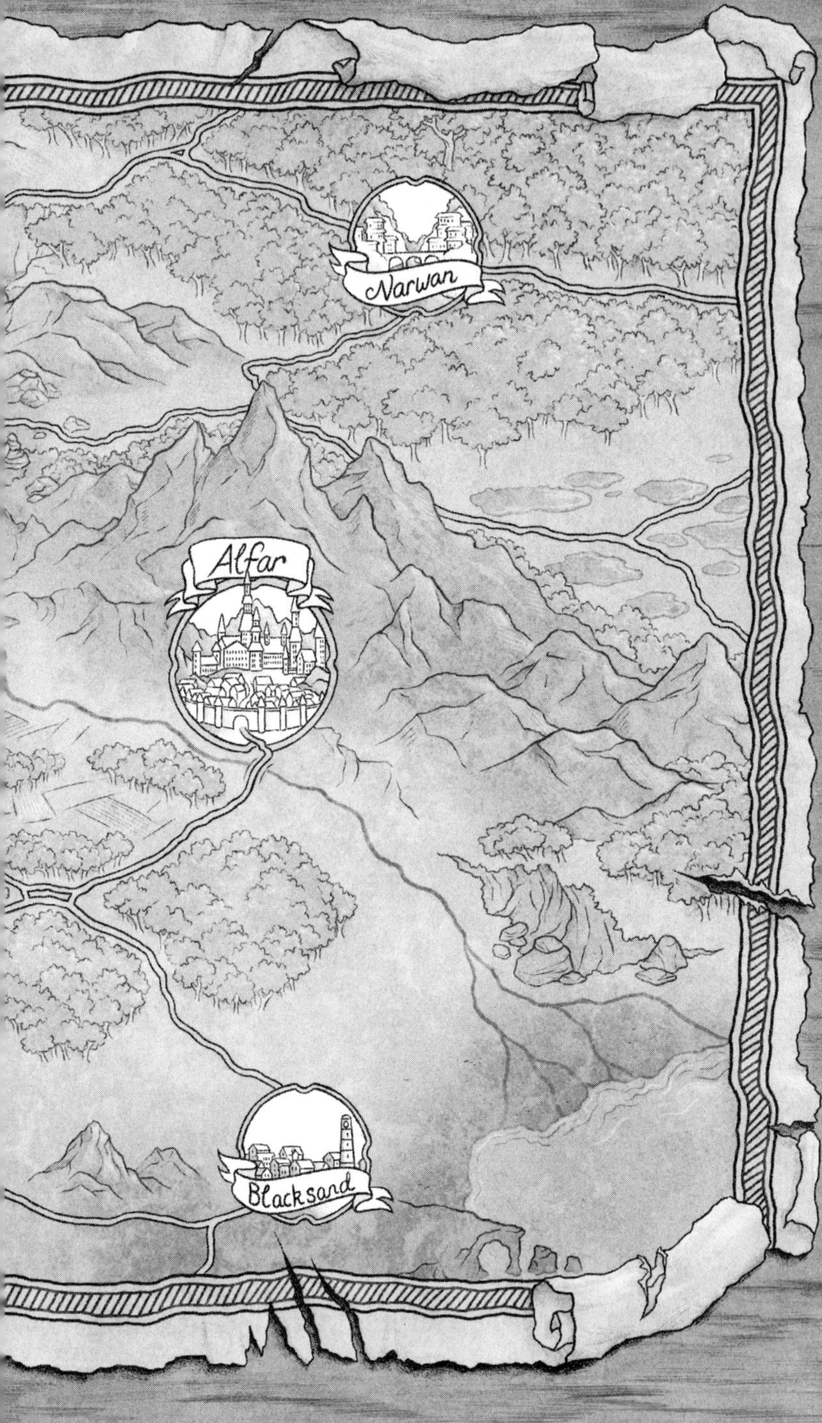
Narwan
Alfar
Blacksand

More from Twinkl Originals...

Continue the learning with exclusive teacher-created resources to engage and inspire children at school, at home and beyond...

This Twinkl Originals storybook is supported by a library of related educational resources, spanning themes and topics covered by the story as well as age-related reading and writing objectives. A variety of engaging, cross-curricular activities, classroom displays, reading comprehensions, writing prompts, adult guidance and more make it easy to integrate exciting literature into children's learning.

Explore the collection at twinkl.com/originals

 Diverse stories, inspiring learning

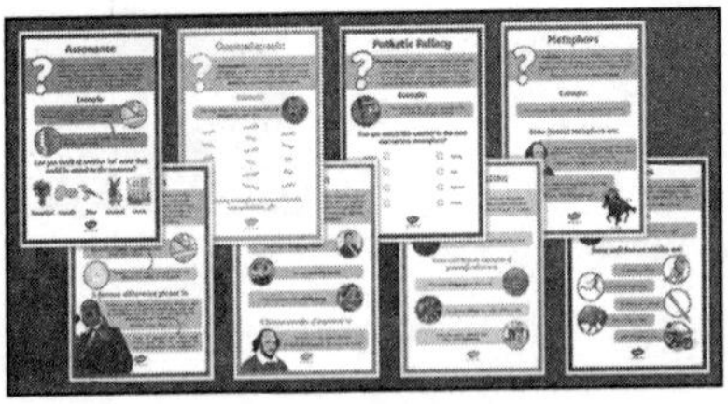
Assonance
Pathetic Fallacy
Metaphors

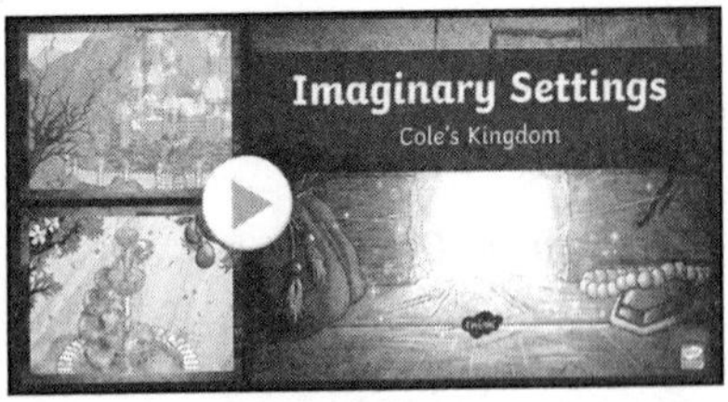
Imaginary Settings
Cole's Kingdom

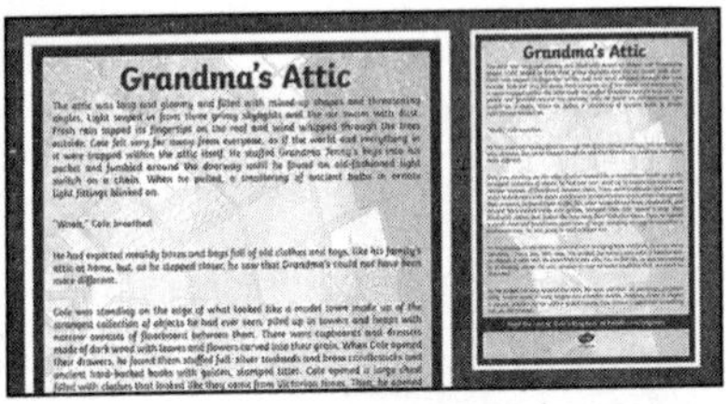
Grandma's Attic
Grandma's Attic

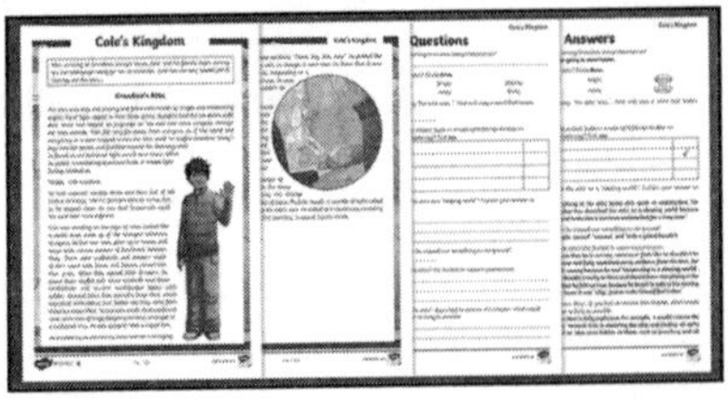
Cole's Kingdom
Questions
Answers

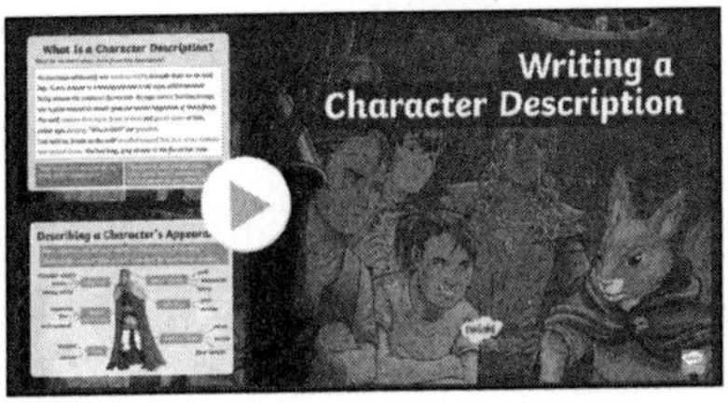
Writing a Character Description
What Is a Character Description?

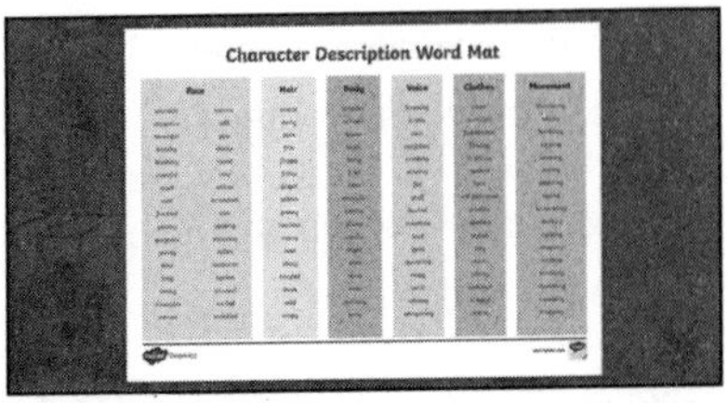
Character Description Word Mat
Face
Hair
Body
Voice
Clothes
Movement

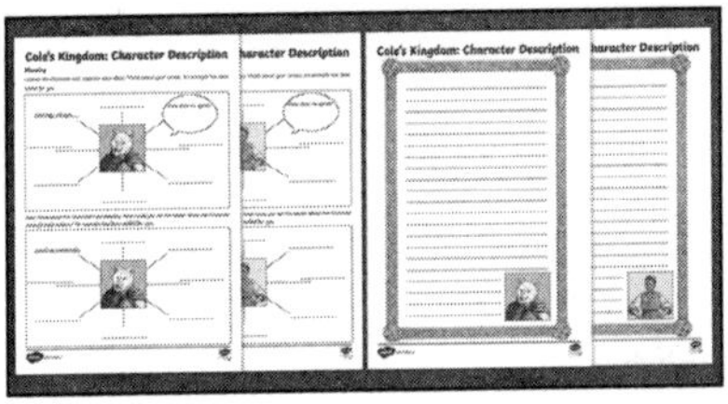
Cole's Kingdom: Character Description
Cole's Kingdom: Character Description

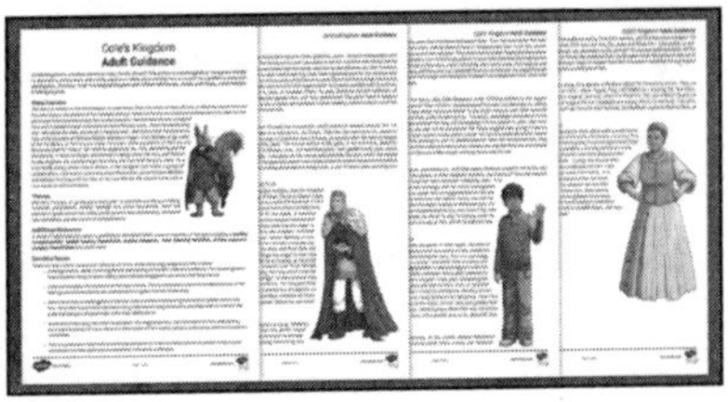
Cole's Kingdom
Adult Guidance

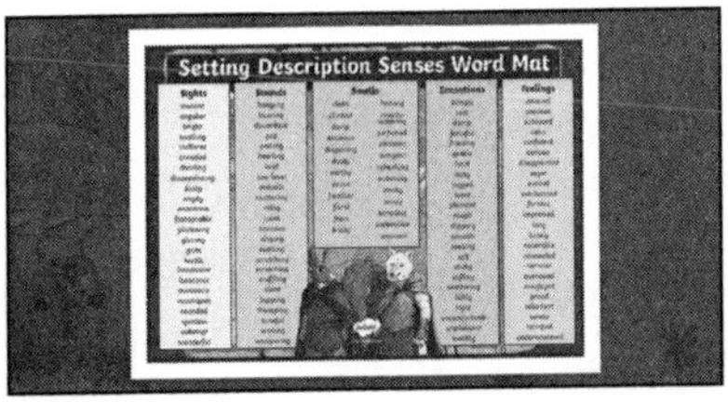
Setting Description Senses Word Mat
Sights
Sounds
Smells
Emotions
Feelings

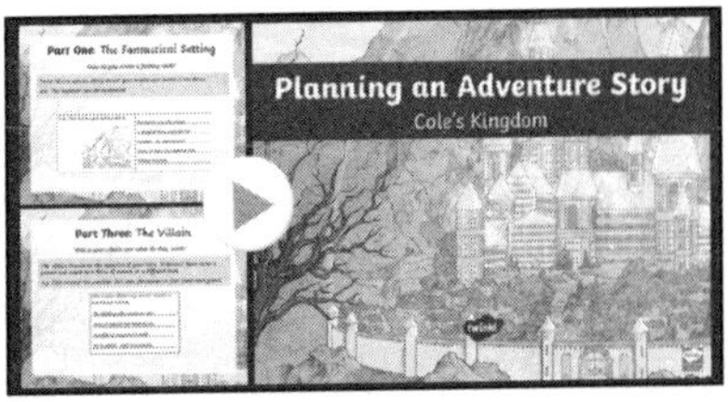
Part One: The Fantastical Setting
Part Three: The Villain
Planning an Adventure Story
Cole's Kingdom

Twinkl Book Club

Twinkl Book Club is a book subscription service.

Enjoy original works of fiction in printed form, delivered to you each half term and yours to keep!

- Twinkl Book Club provides beautifully printed books delivered to your door every half term.

- Professionally written and designed by teachers, created exclusively for use in your classroom.

- Stories reach across the curriculum – every book comes with a range of cross-curricular materials.

- Interactive reading and learning – a powerful way to engage children with stories and reading.

Now for the best part...

Book Club comes as part of a Twinkl Ultimate subscription!

1. Simply sign up to our Ultimate membership.

2. Join the club at **twinkl.com/book-club**.

3. Make your selection – we'll take care of the rest!

The Originals app is here!

Now, you can enjoy Twinkl Originals stories on the move!
Discover a diverse cast of characters in thoughtfully illustrated and expertly written stories that will support learning and encourage a love of reading.

Access the full library of unique Twinkl Originals eBooks, with new titles for ages 0-11+ added regularly.

Multiple user profiles and content controls allow you to personalise your own library of stories. Fully accessible offline – take the library with you wherever you go!

The Twinkl Originals app is available to Apple and Android users.
Search 'Twinkl Originals' in the App Store or on Google Play.